***"You're enjoyi***

Ashe took a step clo
people, shake things up, push people out of their
comfort zone, shock them a bit."

"Well, yes. People come to me because they want
to change, and for that, you have to shake things up.
As a teacher and therapist—"

"I'm not talking about you as a therapist," he
said, taking one more step forward, until he was
absolutely looming over her with his big, powerful
body.

"Oh," she said softly. He was so close she could
smell the scent he was wearing, something dark and
spicy and very, very sexy. She felt little waves of
heat coming off his body. "You mean—"

"As a woman, Lilah," he said quietly, his already
deep voice getting a little deeper.

She gave a little shiver that was part pleasure and
part…okay, no. All pleasure. Nothing but.

Dear Reader,

The idea of the perfect bride, perfect wedding, even perfect marriage persists, even though no woman or marriage could ever meet that expectation.

Which is the reason I found the "Mess the Dress" trend so interesting.

Brides, in their wedding gowns, being photographed rolling in the grass or walking through the ocean? It just seems wrong, even shocking at first, but then the images become compelling, fun, adventurous, freeing.

We will not be perfect brides with perfect dresses or perfect marriages.

We're real women, and we've had enough of trying to live up to that standard.

And as always with things that catch and hold my attention, there's a book idea. In this case, the story of Lilah, a woman who helps women deal emotionally with divorce. She uses her unconventional methods— including "Mess the Dress" sessions—as a way of freeing women from that need to be perfect, to do everything right, to always make the right decisions.

Hope you enjoy it,

Teresa Hill

# MATCHMAKING BY MOONLIGHT

## *TERESA HILL*

**SPECIAL EDITION**

Recycling programs
for this product may
not exist in your area.

ISBN-13: 978-0-373-65671-4

MATCHMAKING BY MOONLIGHT

*Written as Sally Tyler Hayes
†Division One
**The Foleys and the McCords

Other titles by this author available in ebook format.

---

## TERESA HILL

tells people if they want to be writers, to find a spouse who's patient, understanding and interested in being a patron of the arts. Lucky for her, she found a man just like that, who's been with her through all the ups and downs of being a writer. They live in Travelers Rest, South Carolina, in the foothills of the beautiful Blue Ridge Mountains, with two beautiful, spoiled dogs and two gigantic, lazy cats.

A very lucky writer will find herself surrounded by kind, supportive, smart people who make her books better. I count myself very lucky to have at my side my wonderful editor, Charles Griemsman, and agent, Helen Breitwieser.

## Chapter One

Ashe had been warned. The elderly ladies inside were somewhat eccentric, not always reasonable, but supposedly perfectly sane.

It was the *perfectly sane* part that had Circuit Court Judge Thomas Ashford—Ashe to his friends—worried. Why would his friend and longtime colleague Wyatt Gray have included *perfectly sane* in his description, unless Wyatt thought there would be some question about the ladies' sanity?

Wyatt had all but dared him to refuse to help, and Wyatt knew Ashe had a hard time refusing any kind of dare. So before Ashe had fully realized what he'd agreed to, he'd promised to do some vague favor for the ladies inside, something to do with a ceremony of some sort.

The front door of the three-story weathered stone mansion opened, and his first sight of the three little old ladies did nothing to allay his fears.

He'd seldom, if ever, been subject to such a frank appraisal from a woman in her seventies—at least—let alone three of them, and it was more than a little unnerving. One of them seemed quite taken with his shoulders. The middle one just grinned at him. And the third looked as if she was considering testing the strength of his biceps to see if he worked out regularly, which he did. Not that he could imagine why it mattered to her.

He felt like a specimen of some rare and misunderstood species in a zoo.

What in the world were they planning to do to him?

"Judge Ashford, welcome to my home. I'm Eleanor Barrington Holmes," the middle one said, extending her hand to him. "I suspect we've been introduced before, although you may not remember. I believe you know my godson, Tate Darnley."

"From the Downtown Redevelopment Committee? Of course. He's doing an amazing job. Very nice to meet you again, ma'am," Ashe said, taking her hand. "You do a lot of good work for the community."

"I do my best, young man. Please allow me to present my dear friends, Kathleen Gray, Wyatt's late uncle's widow, and her cousin Gladdy Carlton."

"Ladies," Ashe said, shaking each of their hands.

"I'm also Wyatt's grandmother-in-law," the one who liked his shoulders said.

"Such a dear boy, and a delightful husband to our dear Jane," the one who'd looked as if she'd considered pinching him said.

Ashe tried not to look too shocked at that. Wyatt Gray, a delightful husband? That would certainly be a remarkable turnaround for a man who'd been one of the most successful divorce attorneys in the state, a man so cynical about the state of marriage that the idea of him ever entering into it was impossible to believe.

And yet, from everything Ashe had seen and heard, that was exactly what Wyatt had done and he seemed perfectly happy with his choice. Which was even stranger.

"Wyatt said you ladies needed help with a ceremony of some kind?" Ashe asked.

Eleanor smiled up at him. And slipped her hand into the crook of his elbow. "Yes, Judge, that's exactly what we need. Why don't you step out onto the patio for some tea, and we'll tell you all about it."

He let them lead him through several rooms to the patio at the back of the house where they sat down at an ornate black iron patio set. One of the ladies poured him a cup of hot tea, while another set a platter of baked goods in front of him.

"Our dear Amy, Tate's wife, made fresh ginger cookies this morning," Eleanor told him.

Ashe had noticed it smelled wonderful in the house and thought he remembered something about Tate Darnley's wife opening a bakery recently and maybe catering an event Ashe had attended. He took a still-warm cookie from the platter and started to eat. "Excellent."

"Amy does all the baking for our events," Eleanor said. "Weddings, receptions, fundraisers, luncheons, even classes."

So he would at least be well fed if he agreed to whatever the ladies wanted. Judging from the ginger cookies, that was a plus.

"Wyatt tells us you divorce people," Kathleen said.

One of them needed a divorce? He was always surprised when people their age called it quits on marriage, although it did certainly seem that everyone eventually did. Still it seemed as if people would at some point think they were safe from all that, when he'd learned in his job that people never were.

Just the other day he'd had a couple in his courtroom who were ending a marriage after forty-four years. Forty-four years? How could you endure forty-four years and suddenly decide it wasn't working? Had it worked for forty-three years and then stopped? Or had it been kind of bad all along, but not bad enough, until that last year? The last week? Last day?

Ashe really didn't understand.

"I preside over divorces as part of my duties in family court," he said. "One of you needs a divorce?"

"Oh, no. We're not married. It's for a series of classes at the estate—"

"Wyatt said you might be able to help us," Kathleen said.

"Possibly," Ashe said, knowing better than to agree without knowing what he was agreeing to first this time. "What exactly do you need, ladies?"

"A ceremony."

"A divorce ceremony."

Ashe was confused. "We don't really have a ceremony."

"But you could do one, couldn't you? You're a judge. You can marry people, can't you?"

"Well, yes, I'm legally empowered to marry people." Although that was one duty he had yet to perform.

"Fine, just do that in reverse."

Ashe was starting to worry about the *perfectly sane* comments. "It doesn't exactly work that way, ladies. Why don't you tell me precisely what you need."

"A divorce ceremony. Could you make one up?" Kathleen suggested.

"Or we could make one up. I've been divorced," Eleanor said. "I remember everything about my divorce."

"I'm a widow," Kathleen said.

"And I've never been married," Gladdy said.

Ashe helped himself to another cookie, chewing slowly, striving for patience, and then asked, "Why do you need a divorce ceremony?"

"For the classes," Eleanor said, as if that made perfect sense.

Ashe smiled. They were kind of sweet and definitely interesting, but maybe not completely sane. "Ladies, what kind of class requires a divorce ceremony?"

"One for people who are divorced," Kathleen said.

*Of course.*

Why had Ashe even needed to ask?

"So, you're having classes for people who are divorced?"

"Yes," Eleanor said.

Ashe shook his head. "But, if the people coming are already divorced, why do they need to have a ceremony?"

Kathleen frowned. "It may be better if Lilah explains it. It sounds so much better when she does it."

Lilah? Ashe hadn't been warned there was a fourth one. He wondered if the whole concept would sound saner if Lilah explained it. Couldn't sound any crazier, he decided.

"All right," he said. "Where is Lilah?"

"She should be along any moment," Eleanor said.

And that's when Ashe looked up and saw...well, it looked like a mostly naked woman running across the back lawn.

"Oh, dear," Kathleen said. "I so hoped they would be done with all that before you arrived."

"I believe you may be a bit early, Judge," Eleanor said.

"Although I've always appreciated punctuality in a man," Gladdy said, giving him a not at all shy smile.

Ashe was really worried now. One of them was flirting with him, and one of them was nearly naked. He hoped it wasn't the nearly naked one who was supposed to make sense.

"Ladies, I'm not sure if Wyatt told you, but I have to stand for election next year to keep my seat on the bench." Eleanor should understand. She had long been active in local politics, successfully raising money for a number of candidates in addition to her work with various charities. Someone Ashe should know better, he'd been told. Still... "I'm not sure I'm the right man for this job. I'd really like to help you, but someone in my position in the community has to maintain a certain level of propriety—"

"That doesn't sound like any fun," Gladdy said with a smile.

"Gladdy, please," Eleanor said.

She gave a little shrug, not looking at all sorry for her comment. Was she really flirting with him? A man less than half her age? He feared she was.

"I don't think it will be much fun, either," Ashe admitted. "But the election comes with the job. So, if you ladies will excuse me, I'll just—"

"You can't go yet," Eleanor said, grabbing him by the arm. "You haven't even met Lilah."

Ashe was honestly a little afraid to meet Lilah. What if she was even crazier than the rest of them?

"She'll be done soon," Kathleen asked. "And then she can explain everything to you."

Ashe wanted to ask exactly what Lilah was doing but wasn't sure he wanted to know. From what he could tell, someone was on the back lawn of the estate, naked or nearly so, with a long, flowing wedding veil. She seemed to be running around, the glossy white veil trailing after her, and another woman was either chasing her or perhaps photographing her?

Yes, maybe that was it. Now he saw a third person, carrying around some lights on a pole. Photographer's lights?

He hoped so. That was the sanest explanation he could come up with. That what he was seeing was a photo session.

What could a divorce ceremony possibly have to do with the photo session of a scantily clad bride? No matter what, it couldn't be good for a judge facing election soon. People wanted their judges to be above reproach, respectable, steady, solid and, of course, to show good judgment in all things.

Ashe turned his attention from the back lawn of the estate to the three little old ladies with him. He would swear they were trying to look perfectly innocent.

"It's not what you think," Eleanor tried to assure him.

"I have no idea what I think," Ashe admitted.

"And I bet it's been a long time since a woman surprised you," Gladdy said. "We all need to be surprised every now and then, dear."

No, really, he didn't, Ashe thought, smiling uneasily. He liked his life just the way it was.


"Perfect. We got it. Exactly what we wanted." Lilah Ryan lowered her camera with a satisfied sigh. She'd been a budding photographer in high school and through her first year of college, then put it aside for a more practical life, until she realized that being so practical meant losing so much of herself in the process. She wasn't doing that anymore. "Thanks, guys. I really appreciate your patience."

The man carrying the heavy lights for the shoot, Ben—actually her model's boyfriend—groaned as he put the lights down. "Only took twice as long as it was supposed to."

"But we got it right," Lilah said, then turned to the model she'd hired for the shoot. "Zoe, thank you so much. You were great. You're going to look beautiful, I promise. And the posters will be all over town."

Zoe stood tall and slender, the wedding veil wrapped around her, until she slipped into the robe Ben offered. "I don't think they'll let you put these all over town."

"They will, you'll see." Lilah was certain.

The image would be both provocative and tasteful. Lilah would make sure of it. And everyone would wonder what was going to happen at her classes, which was exactly what she wanted.

Lilah had promised herself she was going to do all that she could to get everything she wanted from now on. No more waiting. No more putting aside her own wishes for anyone else. She'd done that for too long.

The three of them picked up their equipment and headed back to the house. It really was lovely, the perfect setting for a wedding. Which also made it the perfect setting for Lilah's classes.

She said goodbye to Zoe and Ben, who helpfully offered to pack up their equipment for her, then went to find Eleanor, whom she called a cousin, but was actually her mother's second cousin's aunt. Eleanor claimed she knew the perfect person to perform the divorce ceremony, and he was supposed to stop by this afternoon.

Lilah was so happy. Everything was coming together just as she'd hoped. She had the perfect location, this beautiful estate where people often came to get married. From her private life-coaching practice, she already had a number of people eager to attend her first series of classes, and now she also had what she was sure would be a striking, provocative image to use on her new promotional materials.

Someone to perform a divorce ceremony would be the icing on the cake.

Some people might think it sounded silly, a divorce ceremony, or a series of classes featuring workshops, group exercises and emotional clearing to help get over a relationship gone bad.

Lilah didn't care. She knew better. She'd learned a lot from the mistakes she'd made in her own life and in dealing with her own divorce. The life-coaching approach wasn't what she'd always envisioned for her career as a therapist, but she was thrilled to be doing this. Over the years, she'd seen too many people doing the same thing, over and over again, stuck in the misery of their current lives and unable to move forward. It had been maddening, frustrating and left her feeling as if she wasn't truly helping anyone.

But now she felt as if she was helping and that this was simply what she was born to do.

Humming happily to herself, she walked through the house until she found Eleanor in the dining room with her two best friends, Kathleen and Gladdy, and a man.

An exceptionally good-looking man.

Not that Lilah really cared all that much how he looked. After all, a woman could only gaze at a man for so long. Eventually he opened his mouth and said something, often something offensive or stupid or simply dull. And then he'd do something controlling or belittling or just plain obnoxious. Looks came to mean so little when the reality of the man set in.

Still, this one was more appealing on the surface than

most, Lilah had to admit. All starch and polish, with a beautifully tailored suit over an equally impressive body. He was tall, broad, powerful, leaning perhaps toward arrogance, but he had great dark hair and beautiful dark eyes.

"Lilah, darling," Eleanor said, beaming at her. "I found the perfect man for you."

"Man?" Lilah backed up a full three inches, not wanting to get anywhere near a perfect man for herself.

"For your divorce ceremony, darling," Eleanor said hastily. "This is Judge Ashford. Judge, my dear cousin Lilah Ryan."

"Oh." Lilah was surprised. "Judge?"

He held out his hand to her. "Ashe, please."

Lilah shook his hand. "I hadn't thought to get a real judge."

"We thought it would lend a nice spirit of authenticity to the ceremony," Eleanor explained. "He and Kathleen's grandson-in-law, Wyatt, went to law school together at Penn."

"Oh, okay," Lilah said, thinking that the judge did not look at all convinced he should help her. "Eleanor explained what I need?"

The judge hesitated, looking from Lilah to Eleanor, then back to Lilah. "A bit."

"It always sounds so much better coming from you," Eleanor said.

It sounded kind of wacky, actually, Lilah had found, but she explained it better than most people. Still, people got married in a ritual. Why was it so odd to use some sort of ritual to mark a divorce?

"It's a series of classes for women who are going through divorce. Actually, most of them are already divorced, they just haven't quite gotten over the relationship. You know, put it behind them, moved on."

"And the ceremony…" Judge Ashford said.

"Is one more way of helping them move on with their lives," Lilah said. "It's really quite simple. Nothing complicated about it. A ceremony to formally mark the occasion. What else can I tell you?"

"Just one thing." He frowned, looking a tad uncomfortable. "Are these women going to be naked?"

"Naked?" Lilah said.

"He saw part of your photo shoot, dear," Eleanor said.

"Oh." *Darn.* That was unfortunate and certainly not the first impression she'd have wanted to send to anyone about what she was doing here.

Still, they'd been on the very back edge of the estate, up against the background of the tall, thick hedges there, so no one outside the estate could have seen them. And if he'd been in the house, from that distance across the expansive back lawn, how much could he have possibly seen? People were practically naked on magazine covers these days and all over TV, after all.

Lilah lifted her face to look him squarely in the eye, feeling distinctly a little huff of judgment and disapproval in the air between them, which got her back up like nothing else these days. And truly surprised her.

How could such a handsome, vital-looking man be so troubled by a woman without her clothes on? Most men, she'd found, were all for naked women wherever they might be found, particularly a woman like Zoe. A young, beautiful, naked model? What could be better than that?

Lilah gave him a bit of that attitude right back. "You have a problem with naked women, Judge?"

Behind her, she heard Eleanor make a sound that was a cross between coughing and choking.

The judge blinked down at her, as he drew himself up even straighter.

Lilah closed her eyes, took a breath and tried to be good. She was looking for his help, after all. "What I meant was… It's not like we're doing a nudist retreat."

The judge studied her even more carefully. "Good to hear it."

And then, Lilah couldn't really tell herself if he was being condescending or was honestly relieved people would be keeping their clothes on. For some reason, she really wanted to know, and sometimes, lately, after years of holding back and being careful and not really saying what she wanted to, Lilah just did. She said exactly what she wanted to, caution be damned.

"I mean, it's not a rule or anything, but it's certainly not what we intend," she told him.

He frowned. "So, you're saying—"

"I don't think anyone will be naked," she said, then couldn't resist adding, "unless they really want to be, of course."

Behind her, she heard Kathleen and Gladdy laugh. In front of her, Lilah saw that she'd brought the judge to a stony silence. She thought she detected the slightest tightening of his jaw, which at this time of day was covered with the faintest hint of stubble, which she admitted to herself was quite attractive on the man. And those dark eyes flashing with a bit of annoyance as they stared at her weren't bad, either.

It occurred to her that perhaps people didn't tease judges as a rule, and she doubted many people had ever mocked him. What a shame. He looked like a man in need of teasing, of loosening up a bit, having a little fun.

She could almost hear her former self saying in her

own head, *Stop playing with the judge, Lilah. He is not enjoying it.*

But honestly, if he was going to be such a stick-in-the-mud about everything, she didn't want him around her students.

She crossed her arms in front of her, smiled as sweetly as she could manage, and said, "So, you do have a problem with naked women, Judge?"

He smiled back, not at all sweetly. Condescendingly, Lilah thought, disapprovingly. "In public, yes. I'm afraid my job demands it."

"What a shame," Lilah said, that sweet smile pasted on her face.

"Oh, stop. She's teasing you, Judge," Eleanor said, jumping in. "Lilah's never once said a word about people being naked here at her classes, and I feel certain she would have mentioned that before we agreed to her using the estate for her work. Lilah, stop toying with the man."

"Sorry," Lilah said, trying to look contrite.

He wasn't buying it.

She was really starting to think people didn't tease the judge.

"I wouldn't want to do anything to make you uncomfortable," she said, looking him right in the eye.

He smiled then, a different kind of smile, an I-understand-you-perfectly smile. Then he leaned toward her and whispered, "I think you like it a lot. I wouldn't be surprised if you're the kind of woman who lives to make people uncomfortable."

Lilah felt a little kick of heat, starting where his warm breath brushed past her ear and slithering through her whole body from head to toe, her senses dancing with delight and that long-dormant hint of sexual interest.

Which honestly freaked Lilah out a bit.

And the judge knew it, damn him. She could tell by the look in his eyes. She'd taken some joy in making him uncomfortable, and he'd very happily done the same to her. Did that mean they were even? That they could stop sparring now?

"I'm…sometimes, I open my mouth and…inappropriate things come out," she said. "Sorry. People will be keeping their clothes on. For everything except, maybe, the destroy-the-dress part of things."

"You're going to destroy dresses?"

He looked genuinely baffled by her. So many people were, and she wasn't sorry. She liked it. She'd been boring for too long.

"Wedding dresses," she explained. "As part of the workshop, women will bring their wedding dresses and… do whatever they want with them. Slash them. Burn them. Roll in the grass with them, jump in the creek along the back of the property…"

"While they're wearing them?" Eleanor asked.

"Yes," Lilah said softly. "I mean, they'll start out wearing them. And then they'll ruin them in any way they want, and…well, I don't know how much people might have left of their dresses when they're done. We want them to feel free to be as creative as they like in their destruction of their dresses. I wouldn't want to stifle any honest expression of emotion. It's therapeutic."

"I'm sure," the judge said.

"It is," Lilah insisted. "I'm just trying to be completely honest here. I suppose there might be some people who really destroy their dresses and might be left…not wearing a lot afterward. So, if it's a deal-breaker for you—"

"Wait," Eleanor said, jumping in. "You two have hardly had a chance to talk, and I'm sure the judge just needs to have a better understanding of the whole concept of your classes. She really is trying to help people, Judge. Lilah's been a successful therapist for years."

He cocked his head sideways at that and just stared at Lilah. She let her nose inch a tad higher and tried not to be offended, knowing he thought she was too flaky to be a highly educated woman, although she had to admit the phrase "successful therapist for years" was definitely an exaggeration.

"She has a PhD in psychology," Eleanor bragged.

"Actually, I have a master's degree, and I'm working on my PhD. The classes are actually part of the research I plan to do for my dissertation," she informed him, although it wasn't something she often mentioned these days unless she was specifically asked about her formal training.

He looked taken aback at that.

Okay, she'd actually been working on her master's degree for nearly a decade and had barely started her PhD classes on the side as her then-husband had pursued his dream of being a college president and they'd moved three times. All of which meant Lilah had changed schools three times and worked full-time at a number of different college administration jobs, putting aside her own dreams and ambitions for a man who, in the end, couldn't even be faithful to her and also couldn't stand the idea of her being more educated and more successful than he was. What a mistake that had been.

"Lilah, darling, didn't you say you have to be somewhere before six?" Eleanor reminded her.

"Yes, I do." No more playing with the judge. Not now. "I have a meeting with the printer who's making my posters for my classes."

"You and the judge should arrange a time to talk later. You can answer all of his questions, give him a chance to make up his mind about this, once he has all the information. Perhaps...over dinner?"

Eleanor beamed at both of them, looking like a woman who was up to something.

"No?" Eleanor said finally, when neither of them seemed happy about the dinner suggestion. "Lunch? Maybe just...coffee? Lilah, darling, give him your business card and take one of his."

They both dutifully produced and exchanged business cards, the judge looking highly skeptical.

"She'll call you," Eleanor promised, then took the judge by the arm. "Let me show you out. We're so happy you could come by today. I'm sure a man like you is so busy. I know Wyatt is..."

Lilah watched the two of them go, then turned to look at her cousin's two partners in crime, Kathleen and Gladdy, both hilarious and outspoken women who seemed to have lived their lives to the fullest. They, too, looked as if they were up to something.

Still, they were just three little old ladies.

How much trouble could they possibly cause?

## *Chapter Two*

Ashe went straight from his odd meeting at the Barrington estate to the law offices of his friend and colleague Wyatt Gray, where he barreled in and found Wyatt frowning over paperwork.

"This is a joke, right?" Ashe said.

Wyatt feigned a look of a complete innocent, something the man hadn't been since grade school at least. "I have no idea what you're talking about."

"This favor you asked me to do?" Ashe glared at him. "It's a joke. It's some kind of payback. I know it is."

"Why would I be setting you up for anything?" Wyatt asked.

"I have no idea."

Okay, maybe Ashe did, because there had been a time when the two men had enjoyed pulling little pranks and generally giving each other a hard time. Like Ashe taking every note Wyatt had on one of his cases from Wyatt's briefcase, leaving him with nothing but completely blank pages on his legal pad and inside his files. It was something Wyatt hadn't figured out until he was actually in front of Judge Whittaker, trying to give his opening argument. The look on Wyatt's face had been priceless.

Or putting red lace panties in his briefcase another time, right before Wyatt was heading to court. He'd nearly choked when he'd opened up the briefcase, again in court in front of the same no-nonsense judge. But still, that was years ago and no proof of any kind had ever been found of Ashe's guilt in either case. They weren't kids straight out of law school. They didn't do this anymore.

Did they?

"You went to Eleanor's, I suppose?" Wyatt asked. "I told you, she can be a little—"

"Strange?" Ashe said.

"Sometimes."

"Your in-laws are even stranger," Ashe insisted.

"They're an interesting group of women. But they're not like…dangerous or anything. I mean, they're all eighty-something—"

"Eighty-something?"

"Yeah. They lie about their ages, all of them. I guess women never really stop. But there are no mental competency issues—"

"What about the one prancing around in the backyard naked?"

Wyatt stopped cold. "Eleanor was dancing naked on the back lawn?"

"No. Not her."

"Kathleen? Gladdy? There's a naked octogenarian at Eleanor's estate?" Wyatt winced.

"No. She wasn't old. She was young. Twenty-something."

"And naked? Really? Naked-naked?"

"She was wearing a wedding veil. A long, sheer wedding veil, but other than that, yeah, she was naked."

"Eleanor let someone have a naked wedding at her estate?" Wyatt laughed out loud.

"No. Not a wedding. Just a woman in a wedding veil, a guy with lights and a woman with a camera," Ashe explained.

"What in the world were they up to?"

"I have no idea," Ashe said.

Wyatt sighed. "See, when I told you those women were...different? This is the kind of thing I meant."

"Random naked women dancing on the lawn?" Ashe was starting to think Wyatt was as puzzled and surprised as he'd been at what had happened. Either that or Wyatt was a better actor than Ashe realized.

"Have you actually had any mental competency testing done on these women?" Ashe ventured.

"No. They're fine, they're the best of friends, just as happy as can be together. And when you have relatives who are eighty-something, you want them to be happy. When they're happy, Jane's happy, and when Jane's happy, I'm happy. We just try to...you know, go along with whatever they want." Wyatt shook his head. "What do they want now? Eleanor said something about classes. I assumed it was something to do with weddings."

"Divorce," Ashe told him. "The classes are about divorce."

"What does that have to do with naked brides?"

"I don't know. They're your relatives. I thought it was some weird setup for a joke. I was sure of it. And now I'm supposed to meet again with Lilah, the one doing the classes, to let her explain everything to me."

Wyatt nodded. "She's a distant cousin of Eleanor's. She grew up here. We actually went to the same private school in first or second grade, Eleanor says, but I'm not sure if I remember her. Her parents moved to Florida ages ago. I don't think she's been back in town long."

"She was the one taking the photos."

"Oh," Wyatt said, then shrugged. "What's she like these days?"

"Eleanor claimed she's working on her PhD in psychology, but I have trouble believing that. And she looks like the love child of two hippies from a commune in the '70s, transported to the present time."

"Oh. I hope she's not...you know, up to something."

"Up to something?"

"I mean, Lilah just popped up out of nowhere, and next thing I know, Eleanor invited her to move in. I haven't had a chance to check her out myself yet. Neither has Eleanor's godson, Tate. We have to be careful. The ladies don't like it when they think we're checking up on them."

"So?"

Wyatt shrugged easily. "If you could just talk to Lilah, figure out what she's trying to do, I'd really appreciate it. I know Tate would, too."

Ashe groaned.

"Hey, you have no idea what I'm dealing with here trying to look after these women," Wyatt complained. "They're manipulative, stubborn as can be, determined to maintain their independence at any price. And it's not like you can twist their arms until they talk. They're little old ladies."

"I'm so happy to hear you're not abusing your elderly relatives," Ashe quipped.

"Remember, this is good for you, too. Eleanor could be a tremendous help when it comes time for your election. That woman knows everyone in this town, and she knows how to raise money. You'll need money, and I know you're going to hate asking people for it."

Ashe groaned. He dreaded the thought of campaigning to keep his job. It was one of the quirks in Maryland's judicial system. Judges were appointed by the governor to an initial term, but to keep their seat on the bench, they had to stand for election. He didn't even want to think about the hassles involved in that. He just wanted to do his job. It was demanding enough all on its own.

Wyatt was right. Eleanor Barrington Holmes was a force to be reckoned with in the community, and he knew she'd helped raise funds for a number of candidates in the past. She could be a tremendous help to him, if she hadn't grown too eccentric of late.

"Come on. Lunch with a woman," Wyatt said. "How hard is that?"

Ashe gave in. "All right. I'll talk to her one more time."

That was how he ended up, on a break from court one day, meeting Lilah Ryan at a little restaurant called Malone's around the corner from the courthouse. He knew almost everyone in the place. They came from the courthouse, because the place was so close, the service was fast and the food wasn't bad.

It was filled with men and women in conservative dark suits, briefcases on the floor beside them, yellow legal pads in front of them as they talked and jotted down notes, cell phones at the ready. Courthouse people. Lawyers and secretaries. A few clients here and there—he could pick them out by the worried looks on their faces. Most people got a little freaked out when they had to go to court.

And there in the midst of all those somber-colored suits was a single blaze of color. Lilah in a soft, silky, flame-colored sleeveless top and a billowy skirt shot through with the same color and lots of others, red to orange to bright yellow. She had sandals on her feet. Her toes were painted the same color as her top, Ashe noted.

Every man in the place was watching her, he realized. Heads kept turning away from legal briefs and legal pads, colleagues and clients, toward her and back again. Clearly, Ashe should have picked another spot for lunch.

Lilah looked up, spotted Ashe, then lifted a hand with flame-colored fingernails and waved. About a half-dozen multi-colored bracelets jangled on her wrist.

He could feel the heads turn from her over to him, see the double takes.

Judge Ashford and the hippie lady?

He made his way to her, stopping along the way to acknowledge friends and colleagues who greeted him with slight smiles, respectful nods of their heads and things like, "Afternoon, Judge."

People respected him here.

He liked that.

He planned to keep it that way.

Ashe got to Lilah's table. She stood and held out her hand, bracelets jangling, and he shook it briefly, waited for her to sit, then sat himself.

"Thank you for taking the time to talk to me," she said. "I wasn't sure you would, but Eleanor insisted no one but you would do for my classes."

He was at a loss. "I can't imagine why. I hardly know her, except for introductions at a charity event here and there. I'm just Wyatt's friend. He's Kathleen's grandson-in-law. He said you might remember him from when you two were children."

Lilah nodded. "Wyatt the wild man? I think he tried to look up my skirt one day on the playground at school when I was six or seven. Or maybe he was the one who dared his friends to do it."

"That sounds like Wyatt," Ashe agreed.

"Is he really married to Kathleen's granddaughter?"

"Yes."

"Happily? I'm so curious about her, but I haven't met her yet. Kathleen said she's written a book—financial advice for women—that's coming out soon, and she's busy getting ready to leave on a book tour. But the idea of the Wyatt I knew being happily married…"

"Well…" Ashe shrugged. What could he say? He had a hard time believing it, too, and he wasn't the only one. He finally settled for saying, "They haven't been married long."

"Hmm. Kathleen and Gladdy believe he's the perfect husband. I would think Eleanor knows better, living in this town as long as she has. But she doesn't say anything when they start talking about how wonderful Wyatt is. I'm starting to worry about all of them. That they might be…you know, not quite all there mentally. Which is such a shame. They seem so nice. A little pushy, a little nosy, but nice."

No arguments with that assessment from Ashe.

"I know Wyatt worries about them. And watches over them quite closely," Ashe added, thinking maybe that would be enough to warn this woman off, if she had any thoughts of taking advantage of some nice, not-quite-there-mentally older women.

"Good," Lilah agreed. "I think someone needs to be watching out for them."

Okay, she was either sincere or she was playing him.

He really couldn't tell, despite what he'd always considered to be really good instincts and people-reading skills.

The waitress arrived. Ashe knew what he wanted and asked if Lilah did as well, telling her they should really go ahead and order, because he didn't have that long before he had to be back in court. She glanced at the menu for all of fifteen seconds and settled on the soup and sandwich special of the day.

The woman got points for being able to make up her mind quickly. So many couldn't, he had found. And she got points for being…not so outrageous today. Maybe this wasn't going to be as much of a chore as he feared.

Then the waitress came back and said, "I almost forgot, ma'am. I asked the manager. He said it's fine to put one of your posters in the window."

She pulled a small poster from her stack of menus and handed it back to Lilah, who smiled and said, "Thank you so much."

Ashe caught a glimpse of the floaty, see-through veil her naked model had been wearing and couldn't believe it. The naked lady on a poster? One that Lilah wanted displayed at the restaurant? Surely the manager hadn't actually taken the time to look at it before agreeing to that.

"You can't put that up here," Ashe told her.

Lilah gave him an odd look. "You heard the waitress. She just said I can."

"A photograph of a naked woman on a poster is not going to work in this town. In fact, I'm sure we have some sort of ordinance against it."

"There's nothing wrong with this photograph," Lilah insisted. "Why don't we let people judge for themselves?" She started to pull a small poster from the envelope she had with her.

"Don't do that," Ashe said, reaching for her. "Not now. Not here."

"Just because you have a problem with a little nudity,

Judge, doesn't mean everyone else here does," she claimed just a little too loudly.

Somehow in their minor tussle, the envelope tore, they both lost their hold on it, and her posters ended up all over the floor, a dozen or so of them, face-up, of course, for everyone to see.

Ashe winced and looked away.

Conversation around them stopped.

People turned and stared, started whispering. There were a few chuckles.

"Does anyone have a problem with this image being displayed here in town?" Lilah asked, holding one up for her audience to see.

Ashe heard mostly male voices, amused and offering no opposition. That was odd. When he turned back to Lilah, she looked quite pleased with herself. She leaned over to pick up her posters, but a number of men nearby had already jumped on that particular task for her, including one of the young waiters, who blushed as he handed them to her.

"Is that you in the picture?" he said, the poor kid's voice cracking and moving up an octave or so.

"No, it's not her," Ashe said, loudly enough for the whole restaurant to hear, because he really didn't need everyone thinking he was having lunch with the naked lady.

Murmurs of disappointment followed from the men in the room. A few speculated about the truth of what Ashe had said, and more than one man said something about wanting to be introduced to the woman who actually was in the photograph.

Lilah thanked her young admirer, then grinned mischievously at Ashe as she set her stack of posters on the table in front of him for him to see. "She might have been naked when I took her photo, but she doesn't look it in the photograph. I'm not an idiot. I do know what I'm doing."

Still skeptical, Ashe looked down at the poster, an advertisement for her Divorce Recovery Classes, and there was the naked woman. Except, well…not quite so naked.

There was the woman Ashe had seen, but shot through the gauzy haze of the wedding veil. Everything was a little fuzzy, so that she looked like a woman running away in a big, billowing wedding veil, but her body was no more than a shadowy impression.

Beautiful, provocative, but still tasteful, he conceded, and certainly that was the intent—to be just provocative enough to catch one's attention and hold it. It was advertising, after all.

Ashe had misjudged Lilah badly, something a man in his profession should definitely not do. Although, honestly, he'd bet she took some devious bit of pleasure in trying to lead him to misjudge her in just this way. The flash of fire in her eyes when he finally looked up at her, that teasing, satisfied smile, told him just that.

"Are you like this with everyone you meet?" he asked. "Or is it just me?"

"I've recently made a vow to enjoy life to the fullest. I didn't for too long," she said. "Besides, most people are much too serious, don't you think?"

"It's a serious world. Serious issues, serious problems. Mine is, at least," Ashe told her.

"Maybe a little too serious."

"Divorce is a serious topic," he argued. "It's really hard for people."

"I know. I want to help them. Truly, I do," she claimed. "If you believe nothing else about me, please believe that. I take helping people very seriously."

"So, tell me what it is you do at these classes of yours,"

Ashe said, deciding she deserved a chance to be heard. Plus, he'd promised Wyatt to find out if she was up to something with Wyatt's wacky relatives.

"Eleanor said you're in family law. Or that you were, and now you hear cases in family court," she began.

"Yes."

"Divorces?"

He nodded. "Plus custody issues both between parents and social services, some probate stuff, guardianship issues for people who are older or incapacitated in some way, that sort of thing."

"Have you seen how some people, while they might have been divorced for a while or just separated for a long time, are still emotionally so entangled in their marriages?"

"Yes."

"To the point of it being highly detrimental to their lives? Clouding their judgment? Keeping them locked into place, unable to move on emotionally or just let go?"

"Yes," he agreed.

He could tell stories that he thought would keep anyone, even the most hopeless, foolish, absolutely blind romantics and optimists, from ever getting married. In fact, he thought if he could videotape some divorce and custody proceedings in his courtroom, he could splice real-life scenes together into a documentary that had the power to end marriage, once and for all, in America, possibly even globally.

"I want to fix that," Lilah said, as she eased back in her seat to make room for the plates of food their waitress was placing in front of them. "Divorced people who can't let go and move on."

"That's all?" He dug into his lunch, deciding she was either supremely confident or hopelessly naive. He thought about telling her his idea for simply ending marriage altogether, which would end the need for helping anyone get over divorce, emotionally or otherwise.

"It's important work," she insisted.

"Yes, it is. I'm just not sure if it's at all possible."

"Well, I intend to try."

She was naive, Ashe feared, perhaps idealistic and completely unrealistic. He felt sorry for her and experienced some small need to try to save her from herself.

"I don't think that's a job for one person, all by herself."

"Then help me."

"I don't think it's a job for two people, either. Way too big for that."

She sighed, sounding disappointed. "Gandhi said, 'Be the change you want to see in the world.'"

Ashe blinked at her. She'd quoted Gandhi to him? "I wonder if he was ever married."

"He was. To the same woman for sixty years," she claimed.

"Sixty years? Truly?"

"He was young when they married," Lilah said.

"Must have been."

"Okay, he was like…thirteen, and she was, too, or maybe a year older. It was an arranged marriage—"

Ashe laughed out loud, truly enjoying that little fact.

"Which has nothing to do with anything—"

"You're the one who brought Gandhi into this," he reminded her.

"Because I admire the sentiment. Imagine what a better world this would be if we all found a problem, a cause we felt passionate about, and went to work fixing it?"

Good grief.

Had Ashe ever been this naive? He didn't think so.

Lilah sighed, clearly disappointed with him. "Please, just think about helping me. I promise I won't tease you anymore about naked women."

Which should have been a plus, he supposed.

"I don't think it's ever a bad thing to try to help people who truly need it," she pleaded. "Watch those people coming through your courtroom and think about whether you believe they need some help letting go, moving on. That's all I'm asking."

He frowned. "You'll be holding these...classes at the Barrington estate?"

Lilah nodded. "It's perfect."

"I thought she'd turned it into a wedding venue?"

"That's what makes it perfect," Lilah claimed. "All that excitement, the anticipation, the happiness. It's like it's in the air there, plus all the physical preparations to turn it into someone's fantasy of the perfect wedding. We get caught up in the fantasy, the dream, and then reality sets in, and... Well, you know all this. You must see it every day. The fantasy doesn't last."

"No, it doesn't."

"I want to use all that energy, all those feelings, the memories. Too often, we try to run away from those feelings or to bury them so deeply we never feel them, and that doesn't work, either. The women coming to my classes won't be able to. Wedding preparations or the dismantling of the wedding fantasies will be all around them there."

"You want to deliberately stir them up?" He saw it now.

Lilah nodded. "Not to be unkind. Just to make it impossible to hide from those emotions. We have to deal with our feelings before we can move on from them."

"So, that's why you're at Eleanor's?" He couldn't argu the sense in that.

"It seemed perfect, once I thought about it. And she' been so kind. She's a good friend of my mother's and distant cousin of some sort."

"And you're living there?"

"For now. I didn't intend to, but I don't know mucl about the town or where I'd really like to live. She offerec and there's so much room there. I'm not a freeloader, i that's what you're thinking—"

"I didn't say anything like that," he protested.

"But you were thinking it. I'm going to see how thing go for me here. If I like it and decide to stay, I'll find m own place. For now, I'm staying in a little room off th kitchen, the maid's room. It's quiet and out of the way an all I really need."

"I'm sorry. I didn't mean to be insulting."

"She's lonely, I think, even with her friends and th weddings. Apparently her godson and his wife and so were living in the guesthouse for a while, but they bough a house and just finished the renovations on it and movec So now it's just Eleanor."

"Well, I'm sure she's happy not to be alone all th time," Ashe conceded, then looked down at his watch He had motions to read before court resumed. "So, that' all you need from me? To perform some sort of divorc ceremony?"

"Well, if it's not too much trouble, there are ofte people in the group who have questions about the di vorce process. They aren't looking for legal advice, bu an explanation of how the process works."

"Okay. I could do that," he agreed.

"And—last thing, I promise—inevitably, I'll run int

a few women whose husbands or ex-husbands are abusive—"

"Yeah, you don't want any part of a situation like that."

"Well, no one does, but it happens, and some of these women will come to me for help."

"Lilah, I see this all the time, and the thing is, a very few of these situations will end very badly, and even I can't predict which ones will. But when it happens, it's really bad, really dangerous."

"I know. I've worked with battered women before. And I know, some cops are better at handling these kinds of situations than others. Some take them much more seriously. I just want a name, that's all. One cop who'll take the situation seriously, and as a judge, I bet you know who the good ones are."

"Yes, I do."

"But you don't want to tell me who they are?"

"No, I think you need a keeper. I don't want to do anything to help you put yourself in the middle of domestic violence situations."

"A keeper? Really?" She looked both amused and mad. "A big, strong man who knows so much better than I do? One I should let make decisions for me?"

"That's not what I said," he told her, although…yeah, he thought it was probably true.

Not because she was a woman, but because she seemed to think she was invincible, ready to charge into even dangerous situations and fix them. Someone should be telling her not to do that, that she was bound to be hurt eventually.

Of course, she obviously didn't want him or anyone else to do that, and she seemed to enjoy provoking him in all sorts of ways.

And it wasn't entirely unpleasant, having her try to provoke him.

"Look," she said finally, "the divorce ceremony doesn't come until the very end of my series of classes, which means the first one won't be for two and a half months or so. You don't have to make up your mind yet. Just think about it."

"All right. I'll think about it," he said.

## Chapter Three

Ashe was wrapping things up for the day in his chambers when Wyatt knocked on his open door. Ashe motioned for him to come on inside.

"Did you really have lunch with a naked woman at Malone's today?" Wyatt asked, looking completely baffled.

Ashe winced. "No, I did not have lunch with a naked woman at Malone's. I had lunch with Lilah, who was fully clothed."

"Oh." Wyatt sounded disappointed, then shrugged at the look Ashe shot his way. "Sorry, it was one of the best rumors I've heard in months."

"Well, it probably has to do with the photograph she took to advertise her divorce classes at Eleanor's estate. I'm sure the posters are all over town by now, if I know Lilah. She wouldn't have wasted any time."

"Oh. Okay." Wyatt frowned but let it go. "So, about Lilah? Do you think I should be worried?"

"I think if those three little old ladies were related to me in any way, I would always be worried," Ashe said.

"True. Pity me, please, and help me. Should I be worried about Lilah?"

"Probably. I mean, I don't think she's a swindler or anything like that. But she likes to shake things up, at the very least. Enjoys it, even."

"Which Eleanor and company will love, if I know them. Are you going to do this class with Lilah?" Wyatt asked. "Please tell me you are, because if you do, you'll know what she's up to."

Which was a great excuse to help Lilah. He could do it for Wyatt. If only Ashe could convince himself that's why he'd be doing it. He thought about how she'd looked today, how vibrant and…interesting.

The woman was nothing if not interesting.

How long had it been since he'd met someone he found truly interesting? Who challenged him the way she did?

"The woman quoted Gandhi to me. 'Be the change you want to see in the world.' What a beautiful world it would be if we all made an effort to try to fix just one problem. She actually said that to me," Ashe added.

Wyatt reminded him, "You try to fix things."

"I do damage control. We all do. You know that."

"Bad day, Judge?"

Ashe nodded.

"Well, do you think Lilah could help people going through divorce?" Wyatt tried finally.

"I don't know. God knows, somebody needs to. There are way too many screwed-up people in the world."

"Look, I'm not asking for a lifelong commitment here. Just do one of Lilah's little classes."

"One class. And you'll owe me big-time."

\* \* \*

Lilah put her posters up all over town, immensely pleased with how well they'd turned out. And—if she was completely honest with herself—how uncomfortable they'd made Judge Ashford.

She got back to the Barrington estate at sunset and found Eleanor, Kathleen and Gladdy just finishing dinner and moving on to coffee and dessert, which they invited her to share. She agreed, having found the trio of women to be delightful, interesting company, although a bit secretive. She always felt as if they were up to something they wouldn't talk about.

"Were you pleased with your little advertisements, dear?" Eleanor asked, as they all dug into delicious fruit tarts with fresh cream.

"I was, but I'd love to hear what you all think," Lilah said, pulling out the last poster, which she'd kept for herself, and holding it up for them all to see.

"Oh, perfect," Eleanor said.

"Absolutely."

"And eye-catching," Gladdy observed. "I hope no one gave you any trouble about them."

"Well, the judge had his reservations, before he'd even seen them. But once he actually looked, he admitted there was nothing blatantly offensive about them."

"Offensive? It's a perfectly beautiful image," Eleanor insisted.

"I thought so, too," Lilah agreed.

"An absolute shame that such a young, good-looking man would be such a prude—" Gladdy began.

"Gladdy, we don't know that. Not at all."

"It certainly seems that way. Someone needs to loosen the man up a bit," Gladdy said.

Lilah tried to hold back a giggle as she thought of how

appealing that sounded. *Loosening up the judge.* Toying with him was one thing. Teasing him, of course. But to truly loosen the man up would require some effort, some action, which she should not undertake. She'd been bad enough the first time they'd met, and she'd had her fun with him over the posters. But she was ready to try to be good.

"Is he going to help you with your classes, dear?" Eleanor asked.

"He's going to think about it."

"Well, I'm sure you can persuade him," Eleanor said. "The women in our family know how to get what we want."

Her smile told Lilah that Eleanor was thinking of more than a woman getting a little help from a man with a divorce ceremony. Apparently all three ladies enjoyed men of every age, body type, personality type, ethnicity and any other attribute Lilah could think of. It had been eye-opening and surprising to hear about their exploits with various men over the years.

Which had left Lilah feeling as if she'd led a very sheltered life. She hadn't admired from afar as many of the men as she should have up to this point, much less actually done the kind of things one didn't do from afar with such men.

Which had her thinking of the judge.

Lilah certainly found it easy to admire so many of his attributes, both physical and otherwise, and she preferred not to do that from afar. Not with him.

"Kathleen, what did Wyatt tell us about the judge?" Eleanor asked. "Single? Married? Divorced?"

"Divorced, Wyatt said. Apparently, they were very young, and the marriage ended years ago."

"Hmm. I was just thinking, if he still had some hard

feelings over his own divorce, that might explain why he seems reluctant to help Lilah," Eleanor said. "Any children?"

"No, none. Wyatt seemed to think he was quite sought-after among the ladies."

"I'd certainly chase him, if I was twenty years younger," Gladdy claimed.

"Twenty?" Kathleen just looked at her.

"It's quite the thing these days, isn't it? The…more mature woman and the younger man?"

Lilah laughed as softly as she could, covering her mouth with her linen napkin, but it was no use. The sound got out, and Eleanor and Kathleen joined her, then finally Gladdy.

"A woman should never be too old to appreciate a good-looking man," Gladdy said.

"Amen to that," Eleanor agreed.

"How old do you think he is?" Gladdy asked.

"Late thirties, I'm thinking," Kathleen said. "He's so distinguished."

"No, mid-thirties. I believe he tries to look and act older than he is, given the job he holds," Eleanor claimed.

"Oh, the joys of a younger man," Gladdy said.

Which set them all to giggling again.

"Things just don't work the way they used to, once a man gets some age on him," Gladdy confided to Lilah. "Such a pity."

"Gladdy, stop," Kathleen pleaded.

"I'm just saying, there are distinct advantages to younger men," Gladdy said. "You should remember that, dear, should you find yourself interested in anyone. So many women go for older men, I suppose for their money or power. But I've always preferred the younger ones. You don't usually have performance problems with the young ones. I wouldn't think the judge would have any problems at all in that regard."

"I'll keep that in mind," Lilah promised. "Although right now, the last thing I want or need is a man."

The estate was scheduled to host an elegant wedding that weekend, and on Thursday evening, Lilah watched as various people came and went, seeing what the house was like as it was prepared for an event.

As the sun went down and the workers setting up chairs, tables and various equipment finally left, she went for a run, and after a quick, cool shower, she put on a comfy pair of pajamas, thankful that the house had quieted down around her.

In the walk-in cooler, she found an opened bottle of pinot noir, left over from a wine tasting with a bride and groom earlier in the week, and poured herself a glass.

She was on her second glass when she glimpsed the headlights of a car illuminating the driveway to the house. Eleanor, coming back from dinner in town, most likely. She thought she heard someone tap softly on the side door. Then, before she could answer it, the door opened, and in walked the judge.

Lilah groaned inwardly and glanced down at her attire.

Cropped pajama pants with a drawstring waist, a little spaghetti-strap top that didn't quite come down as far on her waist as the pants, no bra, no makeup, hair still damp from the shower, two big glasses of wine inside of her.

Then there was the judge, looking all serious and judicial on her, with his perfect, dark suit, a crisp white shirt, dark tie and those lovely, classic dark looks of his. Dark hair, dark eyes, a bit of color to his face that suggested he spent some time in the sun regularly.

"Judge," she said finally. "What a surprise."

He gave her an odd, assessing look. He was holding what looked like a gift-wrapped wedding present, which he placed on the big island in the middle of the kitchen.

"Eleanor said that the side door would be open, that it was fine to just walk in. I was supposed to be at the wedding this weekend, but something came up at the last minute. She didn't tell you I was coming?"

"No, but it's been a hectic afternoon. Lots of people coming and going, getting ready for the wedding." Did he think she'd be here, in her pajamas, if she'd known he was dropping by? "I thought you were Eleanor coming back from dinner."

He shook his head. "I just need to drop off a wedding gift."

"For the daughter of the state assemblyman? You're friends?"

"Yes. We…uh…used to date," he admitted.

"Oh." That was interesting. "No hard feelings, I hope?" Lilah asked.

"She's a beautiful, intelligent woman. I hope she'll be very happy."

"Sorry you're going to miss the wedding. I'm sure it's going to be lovely," she said.

He stood there, hands in his pockets, studying her in the dim light. Nerves got to her once more, and she took a last sip of her wine. He watched her do that, then shifted his gaze to the nearly empty bottle she'd left on the countertop.

"Are you all right?" he asked finally.

"I didn't empty the bottle myself, if that's what you're thinking. It's from a tasting earlier this week, left behind after a half-dozen people sampled it. I'll admit to having a little bit of a buzz, though. Two glasses, and it went straight to my head. I should have just gone to bed."

And then, oddly, she wished she hadn't said the word *bed*.

Although it was true, she should have been there, safe in her bed, instead of here, alone with him this way, feeling vulnerable and sad and underdressed.

"Lilah, I can't begin to figure you out," he said.

"I know." And he really didn't like that. She could tell by the way he said it.

"And I can figure almost everyone out. I have to. It's a very important part of my job. And I'm good at my job. Why can't I figure you out?"

She laughed just a bit. "I'm not sure I understand myself that well, which is not a good thing. I'm not sure I'm...fully formed the way a woman my age should be...."

*Oops.* There she went again. *Fully formed? Really, Lilah.*

"See, right there. I can't tell if you're deliberately trying to be provocative or not."

"No. Not this time," she said. "I admit, I have...baited you in the past, and I'm sorry for that. I mean...I know I should be—"

"But you're not sorry—"

"No. You just seem so...uptight." There, she blurted it out.

"I'm not," he argued. "I just happen to hold a very public position in the community, and there are things expected of me and my behavior."

"Of course."

"And you, from what I've seen, are a woman who prides herself on being as outrageous as possible—"

"No. Really, I don't. I just...I want to be me, and not

some buttoned-up, repressed version of me to please someone else."

"I am not repressed," he said with a bit of heat, clearly enunciating each word.

"No, I wasn't talking about you. I was talking about… someone else. Someone who did that to me. Or…no, I did that to myself, because it was my choice, and now, I choose not to do that anymore. I choose to be me, and I'm not changing for anyone. I promised myself that."

He leaned back and studied her once more, shaking his head back and forth.

"I'll try to be good from now on, I promise," she tried.

"And there you go again. What are you doing?"

"Trying to apologize, to say I'll stop baiting you." She laughed a bit, couldn't help it. Something about this man…

"You're enjoying this!" He took a step closer, which actually put him a bit too close for comfort. "That's what I keep thinking, that you know exactly what you're doing. I think you like to play with people, shake things up, push people out of their comfort zone, shock them a bit."

"Well, yes—the shake things up, push people out of their comfort zone part is true. People come to me because they're uncomfortable with their lives. They want to change, and to bring about change, you have to shake things up. As a therapist—"

"I'm not talking about you as a therapist," he said, taking one more step forward, until he was absolutely looming over her, crowding her, trapping her between the kitchen cabinets and his big, powerful body.

"Oh," she said softly, when he was so close she could smell the scent he was wearing, something dark and spicy and very, very sexy. She could have stood there, happily, taking in that scent and feeling little waves of heat coming off his body for a long, long time. "You mean me…"

"As a woman, Lilah," he said quietly, and his already deep voice got a little deeper and a whole lot sexier.

She gave a little shiver that was part pleasure and part…okay, no. All pleasure. Nothing but.

But *toying* with him?

Was she really?

She thought about it. She liked him, or liked poking at that very serious side of his to see if there was another side, a more fun side.

Was that *toying?*

Was it…too intrusive? Kind of mean? Annoying?

He wasn't a patient, a student or even a friend. An acquaintance at best.

"Is it really so bad?" she asked him.

He growled, looking even more irritated with her. "Okay, just tell me. Is this some kind of come-on? Are you trying to start something?"

"No," she said, honestly surprised and puzzled at that. "I don't think so."

"You don't think so?" he repeated. "I don't know if I can be any clearer about the question. Are you trying to let me know you're interested in me and to find out if I'm interested in you? Because, if that's what it is, just say so. It might be…interesting."

"Interesting?" She wasn't sure at all how to take that. *Strange? Amusing? Distracting? What?*

"No, I'm certain it would be interesting," he decided. "I'm just not sure it would be wise—"

"Fine," she said. So it would not be smart to have anything like that to do with her? Gosh, he might have some fun. However would he handle that? "I'm fairly certain it's not a come-on—"

"Fairly certain?" he repeated again.

"I…I…I had to think about it," she said, practically tripping over her own words with nerves and maybe a hint of excitement, even anticipation. *Damn.* "I might have to think about it a little more before I'm absolutely sure. But you put me on the spot, and I did my best to give you an answer. I'm fairly certain I'm not coming on to you or trying to start something with you because… Well, just because… You're really not my type…anymore."

"Fine," he said, as if it wasn't fine at all. And then he leaned in closely enough that, for a moment, his mouth was only a breath away from hers, and said, "Let me make myself absolutely clear. I'm not a toy. Stop playing with me."

"Well, if you insist," she said, feeling something she could only label as regret. Over no longer *playing* with the judge? She looked him up and down, taking in the near scowl on his handsome, tanned face, the beautifully put together body, the sense of leashed power that seemed embedded in him at all times.

Maybe she had been coming on to him, like an unconscious reflex or something… Some need to try out her newfound freedom or just…feel like a woman again.

"See, right there," he said, not backing up an inch. "You're doing it again. Teasing, trying to provoke me."

"No, I'm not. If I was truly trying to provoke you, I'd tell you that the little old ladies who live here spent their afternoon teatime telling me that someone needed to loosen you up—"

He groaned.

"And I'm pretty sure they think the person to do that should be me, though I have no idea why. Maybe they think it would be amusing to watch me toy with you—"

"Lilah, I swear, if you don't—"

"And if I really wanted to mess with your head a little bit, I'd tell you that Gladdy spent the afternoon telling me about the...frustrations of dating a man of a certain age—"

"What could that possibly have to do with me?" he asked.

"That they have certain...performance issues..."

He looked both angry and a little bit horrified.

"You're telling me that you and an eighty-something-year-old woman have been speculating about what I can or can not do all on my own in the bedroom?"

"Not me," she insisted. "Gladdy. It was all her."

"Unbelievable," he said, still right up in her face, so angry, so very handsome.

He was breathing hard, his breath warm with a hint of mint as it fanned over her face, her mouth. His body was also so warm, and it had been so long since she'd been this close to a man, one she truly found attractive, even if he was maddening.

Part of her just wanted to cuddle up against him and enjoy all the warmth, the strength and solid bulk of a man. She was swaying toward him, she feared, and maybe... just maybe, he was swaying toward her, as if there was some kind of invisible force field between them, drawing them together.

She wasn't sure if he was the one who moved closer or if she was, but she caught her breath at the contact, at how deliciously sexual it felt and how much she found herself wanting him in that moment.

He felt it, too.

She knew he did.

No hiding from it.

He either got a little turned on, arguing with a woman,

or he wanted her… Okay, more than a little bit turned on, from that momentary brush of his body against hers.

Because he was most definitely aroused.

Gladdy was right, no pharmaceutical help necessary.

Lilah had been staring at the pattern of his tie, avoiding his gaze at all cost, but she finally gave in and looked him in the eye.

"Well, now you know. Satisfied?" he growled at her as he eased away.

*No, not nearly.*

But for once, she managed to hold her tongue, as he turned and walked away.

## *Chapter Four*

Ashe had a terrible case to handle on an emergency basis that Friday and Saturday, wrapping it up late that afternoon, and he had instructions to report to his boss, the administrative judge, on the outcome, as soon as the case was finished. As luck would have it, that judge was at a certain wedding that weekend, where his second wife's niece was getting married.

A place where the most outrageous woman Ashe had ever met—no, the two most outrageous women, if he included Gladdy—also happened to be, making it the absolute last place Ashe wanted to be, except for the room at the hospital where he'd heard his latest case.

The reception sounded as if it was in full swing, as Ashe entered through the side door that led to the kitchen, where he'd found Lilah in her pajamas two nights ago.

He was relieved to see that she wasn't there today.

The catering staff was clearing plates and cleaning up

as he walked through the kitchen and followed the noise to the expansive stone patio where a number of guests still remained, drinking, eating and dancing.

"Judge, I thought you wouldn't be able to join us today," Eleanor said as she approached him.

"I'm not," he said. "I just need to talk to Judge Walters for a moment. Court business. Do you know where he is?"

"I'll find him. Why don't you wait for him in the study? It's nice and quiet there. I'll take you."

"Thank you," he said, following her down the hall, down another one and then into a blessedly quiet private room.

"You look tired. And I imagine you've had a difficult couple of days," Eleanor said. "Judge Walters and I are old friends. I believe I know the case he handed you."

"I'm sorry, I'm not supposed to talk about it," Ashe said.

"Of course not. Have you eaten? We have plenty of food. I'd be happy to send someone with a dinner plate for you," she offered.

"I'm fine, Eleanor, thank you. I'm just going to talk to the judge and go home."

"Well, I'll send him right away."

Lilah forced herself to watch the wedding and reception. She'd also stayed away from the wine, so her head was perfectly clear when Eleanor asked her to deliver a dinner tray to the study.

"Of course." Then Lilah wondered why a server wasn't handling this particular job. "Eleanor, who's in the study?"

"A tired, hungry man who's just finished a very difficult job. Be nice to him," she instructed.

"I will, but why am I doing this?"

"Because when the man he's with right now leaves,"

he'll be all alone, and you'll be able to apologize in private."

"I can't do it," Lilah cried. She'd confessed some of what she'd said and done with the judge the night before to a delighted Eleanor that morning. "I can't face him."

"You can, and you will. He's a judge, darling. He's heard everything."

"But I'm not one of his court cases. He's not required to be fair, reasonable or impartial to me."

"Lilah, dear, I told you, he's tired, hungry and in need of a little comfort at the moment—"

"Comfort? What exactly do you mean, comfort?"

"I'm not asking you to walk in there and take your clothes off. Just be nice to the man. He had a bad day."

"But I don't think he finds anything about me comforting," she said.

"Well, do your best, dear. It's fine and good to challenge a man, to throw him off balance a bit, but sometimes a man needs a sympathetic ear and a soft touch."

"Now, see…touching him is definitely not a good idea."

"I've seldom found that putting one's hands on a handsome man is a bad idea," Eleanor claimed, as they got to the study door. "Don't be a coward, dear. Tell the man you're sorry, give him his dinner and let him tell you about his day. This silly misunderstanding will be forgotten in a moment. And reassure him that Gladdy's not here. I sent her home with Kathleen."

There was a plus. No Gladdy. Still…

"I didn't tell you everything," Lilah admitted. "He made it clear that he wants me to leave him alone."

Eleanor dismissed that notion with a wave of her hand "He's a man. A very handsome man, and you're a lovely woman. I'm sure he didn't mean it."

"He said it wouldn't be wise to get involved with me," she added.

Eleanor laughed. "My dear, surely you don't believe men are always wise in their involvements with women."

"He was absolutely clear," Lilah said, trying again. "He said, 'I am not a toy. Stop playing with me.'"

"Then stop playing," Eleanor said.

*Stop playing?*

Lilah fell silent.

That was Eleanor's advice?

She would have protested even more, but she heard the doorknob to the study turning. Eleanor looked positively triumphant for a moment, then hurried away. Which left Lilah just outside the door as it opened, and out came an elderly gentleman, who'd been in the midst of congratulating the judge on a difficult job done well.

"Ah, the veal. It was excellent," the older man said, studying Lilah. "Do we know one another, young lady? I'm Judge Walters. The bride is the niece of one of my former wives."

"I don't believe so, sir. I'm Lilah Ryan, Eleanor's cousin."

He nodded, then asked, "The woman on certain posters all over town?"

"No, sir. I'm the one who took the photograph."

"Ah, the one from lunch that day with the rascal in there?" He nodded back toward Judge Ashford.

"We did have lunch one day," she admitted.

"Don't believe a word he says," the older man whispered to her. "The man goes through women like there's an endless supply of good ones, all wanting to put up with whatever nonsense he dishes out. Remember that."

"I will, sir," Lilah promised. "But, honestly, I just came to bring him dinner. Eleanor insisted."

"Ashford, eat the dinner this fine-looking young woman brought you, have another glass of Eleanor's husband's private supply of bourbon and forget all about your case," the older man said, then left.

No one but her and the judge then. She glanced at his face, finding it nearly unreadable. Tired? Frustrated? Angry? Surprised, and not in a good way? All possibilities.

"The veal really is exceptional." She held out the tray, waiting to see if he let her into the room.

He finally did. She put the tray on the desk, beside two empty glasses and a bottle of bourbon.

"That man is my boss. I think it was a direct order that I have another drink and eat."

Lilah poured him another drink, put down the bottle and then worked up every bit of her courage she could find to say, "I really am so sorry about the other night. Could we just…say that I was drunk and leave it at that?"

He sat down in one of the chairs in front of the desk, took a bite of the veal, made a sound of utter appreciation after he chewed and swallowed, then looked at her. "You said you weren't drunk."

"Well, how many people are honest about whether they're drunk?"

"Not many," he admitted. "But people usually claim they weren't intoxicated when they really were. I don't think you were."

"Okay, I wasn't. I'm just… You have to believe the last thing I wanted to do was to have to face you again, and the only reason I'm here now is that Eleanor made me do this."

He took another bite of his dinner, clearly enjoying it and possibly Lilah's apology. "She made you?"

Lilah made a face. "She called me a coward."

He laughed then. "I imagine you don't let anyone get away with that."

Then he went back to his dinner, absolutely attacking it. Obviously, he was hungry. At least Lilah had made him laugh, even if he was laughing at her.

"Shut the door and sit down," he invited, after she'd hovered by the door for a long moment trying to figure out what to do.

"Are you sure? It's no telling what I might say," she warned him.

"Well, I won't say I'm not...uneasy about the possibilities, but with the door closed, this room is wonderfully quiet, despite all the commotion from the reception, and I'd really appreciate the quiet and the privacy. If I ever have to come face to face with Gladdy again..."

"She's not here."

"Good."

Lilah shut the door and sat in the other chair facing the desk.

"Can I get you anything else? There's more veal, if you want it, or a piece of the wedding cake?"

"No, thank you. This was perfect." He put his fork down, wiped his mouth with the cloth napkin and covered the tray with it. Then he sat back and sipped his bourbon.

"Eleanor and Judge Waters said you had a bad day, a difficult case," she said.

He nodded.

"Can you talk about it?"

"I'm not supposed to discuss the cases before me, but this one's been in all the newspapers. The girl's lawyer made sure of that, no doubt wanting the publicity. So the facts of the case certainly aren't a secret. A fifteen-year-old cancer patient sued her parents for the right to make her own medical decisions. Her doctors say there's little meaningful chance of a cure at this stage, and she wanted the right to stop treatment and go home. Her parents weren't ready to give up."

"That's horrible," Lilah said.

"Yeah, it is."

"I never imagined you having to deal with anything like that."

"Thankfully, I seldom do." He took another slow sip of his drink.

"So, how do you go about deciding a case like that?"

"The law offers the vague, rather unhelpful guideline of what's in the best interests of the child."

"And you're supposed to decide that? When the girl and her own parents can't?"

He nodded.

"So, what did you decide?"

"I didn't. Not really."

"So, who did?"

"As you'll no doubt be able to read tomorrow in the papers, her parents agreed to take her home. Case dismissed," he said carefully.

"You got them all to agree, when no one else could?" she guessed.

"It's my job, Lilah."

"So, why did you decide to convince them to take her home?"

He looked her right in the eye. "I didn't say I did."

"Not exactly, but that's what you did." She was sure of it.

"Look, I'm not supposed to talk about specific cases," he began.

"Of course. Sorry."

"It's okay. In general, you just watch and listen. That's really all you can do. Who do you believe? Sometimes, you have to determine who has the necessary education and expertise to speak on the subject at hand. And who should get to decide."

"Well, I would think that would be the hardest part of all. Who should get to decide?"

He nodded.

She wanted so much to ask him how he came to that decision but didn't want him to break his own rules.

"Look, I wish everybody could make good decisions on their own all the time," he said. "But sometimes, people just can't. They're too afraid, too sad, too angry. For whatever reason, they can't see the situation clearly and have no hope of being objective. They need someone to do it for them, especially when all the answers are lousy ones, like this one. She goes through yet another highly toxic treatment and probably dies, or she goes home and probably dies."

Lilah nodded. Definitely no good options there.

"And if blaming me for the decision makes it easier for her parents to take her home, probably to die, I'm okay with that. Not that she'll be gone, but it's not within my power to stop that. Just that…it's what she wants, and she's been through enough to know exactly what stopping treatment means."

Still, it was an awful burden to carry, Lilah thought. And he seemed so calm, so sure of himself. "How do you know you did the right thing?"

"You don't ever know for sure. Not really. I mean… unless you were spectacularly wrong and something disastrous happens. You send a kid back home when social services had removed him from his parents' care, and he ends up in the hospital. Or worse. Then you know. You really screwed up. But most of the time…you just have to do your best and hope you're right in the end."

He closed his eyes and shook his head. "It was the damnedest thing. We talked for a while, just the two of us, and she just seemed so normal in so many ways, in spite of all she'd been through. One of the things she wanted more than anything was to look pretty, to look normal. Such a typical thing for a teenage girl to want."

"Her hair had fallen out?" Lilah guessed.

"Yeah. I guess wigs aren't very pretty, at least if you're a teenage girl. And I have definitely said more than I should have now. It just struck me how normal she was to be worrying about something like that, and yet, at the same time, in court asking for permission to go home to die."

Lilah shook her head. "That's awful. I can't believe I've been giving you a hard time about…silly things, when you have things like this to deal with. I'm so sorry."

He shook his head. "Forget it. It's nothing. You're just…a puzzle, but not an entirely unpleasant one."

*Not entirely unpleasant?*

Definitely not the nicest thing a man had ever said about her, but she'd take it.

"That's why you missed the wedding? You knew you had to deal with that case? That night when you came over to drop off the wedding present?"

He nodded.

She groaned. "Now I feel even worse about the whole thing."

"Don't. I wasn't in the best of moods, and I thought… I'd told Eleanor I was going to drop by, and when I saw you in the kitchen in your pajamas…"

"She didn't tell me you were coming, I swear."

"I believe you."

"And even if I knew you were, I wouldn't have the nerve to be there waiting for a man in my pajamas, especially one who has no interest in seeing me in my pajamas—"

"I never said I didn't want that," he claimed.

"Yes, you did." She'd heard him.

"No, I didn't. I said I couldn't tell if you were coming on to me or not. I still can't, by the way."

Lilah blinked up at him as he leaned back in the chair sipping his drink and staring at her over the top of the glass.

"You told me to stop playing with you," she reminded him.

"Yeah, I did. I didn't want to do something you didn't want because I'd read you wrong."

"And you said it wouldn't be wise to get involved with me."

"You think it would be?" he shot back at her, as he finished his drink and stood up, putting it on the tray of food and pushing the whole thing to one corner of the desk.

"No. Probably not," she admitted. "I just…I didn't think it was an option, because…I thought you weren't interested…."

"Do you remember how our conversation ended the other night, Lilah?" He spoke slowly, carefully, as he sat on the edge of the desk now, watching her every move.

His body brushing against hers…

*Now you know,* he'd said. *Satisfied?*

"Okay, I missed that," she said.

He shot her a challenging look.

*Missed that?* "No, not that. I couldn't possibly have missed that," she rushed on, blushing just remembering. "I mean…I think I may have trouble reading you, too, Judge."

## Chapter Five

"Ashe," he said softly. "My friends call me Ashe."

She watched as a slow stamp of satisfaction came across his face.

*Well, wasn't that interesting?*

The look he gave her set her whole body to tingling. He reached out a hand to her, and she put her hand in his, her heart thudding wildly all of a sudden. With a little tug, he brought her to her feet, eased back a bit onto the desk and pulled her to stand between his thighs. With him sitting like that, they were eye-to-eye, mouth-to-mouth.

"Ashe," she said, liking the sound of it. It fit him. Dark, all banked fire and smoldering heat somewhere deep inside.

He ran his hands up and down her arms easily, softly, giving her time, she thought, to object if she wanted to or maybe just to savor the moment that was to come.

She put her hands against his chest, not to keep him

away but just to be able to touch him. She slipped her fingers beneath his suit coat, against his shirt. He smelled so good, and his body was solid and wonderfully warm. She remembered wanting to just snuggle up against him the other night and have him hold her.

She wanted more than that now.

He watched as he used the back of his finger to brush up her bare arm, along her collarbone, to her chin and then along her jaw, to her ear. He slipped his hand into her hair, cupping her head. His other hand was at her waist, urging her body more tightly against his. She sucked in a breath, and the movement sent her breasts flush against his chest.

"I can't decide where to start, what I want to taste first."

That sent a shiver all through her body, because he both acted and sounded like a man with all the time in the world, and she was his own, personal feast.

Lilah didn't think anyone had ever feasted on her before. Not in leisurely fashion or in any great detail, at least. It felt as if her legs had turned to jelly. She clutched at his shoulders and leaned hard into him for support, and because the feel of his big, hard body against hers was so very enticing.

He finally kissed her softly, slowly, maddeningly on her mouth and then licked at her lips with his tongue, and it was absolutely delicious, the sweetly enticing taste of him. She tried to be patient, to let him do what he wanted, because it was divine. He teased at her ear with his tongue, his warm mouth, at her collarbone, her neck, slowly, deliberately.

Where did he find the patience? Lilah wondered. She wanted to devour him whole. If not for the unmistakable reaction of his body, pressed intimately to hers thanks to the hand he had low on her back, she would have thought the man was calm as could be.

But he wasn't. He wanted her badly, and she wanted him, just like that. She was rocking her hips against his at that very moment, telling him so, whimpering like a woman desperate for him.

And he was smiling as he toyed with his mouth along the edge of her top as it lay over the curves of her breasts.

She took his head in her hands and held him to her, easing back in his arms, gasping as his mouth closed over her nipple right through her clothes. She felt the heat of his breath, his mouth, the slide of his tongue, and then a little nip with his teeth that went through her like a bolt of lightning, leaving her whole body throbbing with desire.

And still, he moved so slowly and deliberately, while all her nerve endings were screaming.

He got his mouth beneath the neckline of her top, pushed her breast up with one hand and then he had his mouth on her with nothing in the way, ratcheting up the sensation even higher.

When he finally lifted his head, his eyes were darker than ever, smoldering, and he said, "I want to lay you across this desk, strip you naked and taste every inch of you. Does that door have a lock?"

She just blinked up at him. She was supposed to think? Now? When he'd just told her what he wanted to do to her?

"I…I don't know."

"We need a locked door." He stood up, holding her by the waist, and reversed their positions, until she was the one sitting on the edge of the desk. He left her long enough to check the door. He sounded very, very pleased when he said, "Oh, yes, it does."

She heard the slight click of the lock falling into place,

and then he was back, standing in front of her, using his arms to bring her body back flush with his.

"You look nervous," he said, watching her.

"A little."

"Or scared? Which one?" he wanted to know.

"I…both, I guess. A little of both."

"I'll stop," he promised. "It's fine. I just need…more. Just a little more, Lilah."

She nodded. Nervous or not, scared or not, she definitely wanted more.

He took her mouth in his again, seriously this time, no teasing at all. Like he was indeed intent on eating her up. She gave as good as she got, she hoped, opening herself up to him, locking her arms around his shoulders, her legs around his hips as he leaned into her.

He murmured his satisfaction with that particular move, then tore his mouth from hers and went searching for her breast again. This time he yanked her top up, until he'd uncovered one breast and laid siege to it once more with his mouth, sucking strongly in time with the thrust of his body against hers.

It was absolutely delicious, Lilah decided.

Devouring her…

So, this was what he'd meant.

She pulled her top and her little skimpy bra up and over her head in one motion, dropping it somewhere, and reveled in the heated satisfaction stamped across his handsome face. Then she eased back on the desk, wanting to feel the weight of his body on top of hers, and he followed her down. It felt so very good, and Lilah was wondering if she truly did want him to stop, if he…

Her head brushed along something.

A glass, she realized, as she heard it dance across the desk and then shatter against the hardwood floors.

Ashe must have reached for it, because the hand that had been slowly easing her back to the surface of the desk disappeared. She reached out, too, instinctively, feeling herself falling without his support. And one of them, maybe both of them, hit both the glass and the tray of food.

All of it went clattering absurdly loudly against the floor.

Crystal shattered, as did china. The silverware seemed to skitter along the wood at first, before finally settling into place and falling silent. And the tray... That had to be the weight of the tray making that horrendous, final crash.

Lilah lay back against the top of the big, wooden desk, reaching for her top which was nowhere to be found. Ashe loomed over her, breathing hard and swearing softly.

"I'm sorry," he said.

"No, it was me. Do you think anyone—"

Before she even got the question out, she heard the door open. How could the door be opening just like that?

A woman's voice said, "Is everything all right in... Oh. Sorry."

Lilah closed her eyes and leaned into Ashe's chest, hiding and hoping no one could see her face at least. Then she heard footsteps, more than one set.

Eleanor said, "I hope no one was hurt by the breaking glass."

"We're fine," Ashe said. "We'll take care of—"

"Oh. Oh, my dear," Eleanor said. "I'm afraid the lock on that door has never worked."

And then laughter, little bits of laughter here and there.

"How the hell many people are in the hall?" Ashe whispered to Lilah. He slipped his arms around her and lifted her up so she was no longer lying on the desk but upright, and he shifted his body, angling it toward the door, shielding her as best he could.

"I don't know," she whispered back, hiding her face against his chest.

"Could someone shut the door, please?" Ashe asked, showing a hint of a man used to giving orders and having them obeyed.

"Of course," Eleanor said. "I am so sorry."

Lilah waited there, pressed against him, until the door closed and the laughter and the footsteps receded. Then she just stayed there snuggled against him, his arms around her, enjoying the heat of him, that lovely, manly smell. She didn't want to move.

He groaned, took a breath and absently rubbed his hand up and down her back for a moment. It made her think once again of how deliberately he moved, kissed, seduced. Where did he find the patience? It was both maddening and wickedly arousing, frustrating and devastating.

"I'm sorry, Lilah," he said softly, then waited until she finally lifted her head to face him. "I shouldn't have done that. Not here in the midst of all these people."

"Me, too," she agreed.

"I forgot all about the glass and the tray—"

"So did I. Could you... Do you see my top anywhere?"

"Sure." He eased away from her, bent down to scoop it up off the floor in front of the desk and handed it to her. "Wait, I think this is yours, too."

He handed her the tiny bit of a bra she wore.

It was a little stretchy thing, which she pulled over her head and into place. She caught him watching as she dressed. "What?"

"I wondered...if you wore one," he admitted sheepishly. "Not much to it. Not that I mind at all. I just...wondered."

She slipped her top over her head and into place. "I never thought I needed much of one."

"No...I mean... Some of those things seem so...harsh and...overly controlling. I mean, is it really that hard to contain those things? It's not like they're trying to run away or something."

"Mine have never tried to get away from me," she told him.

He finally stopped looking at her breasts, and then they just looked at each other.

"So, this is awkward," she said finally. "How many people saw us?"

"I'm not sure."

"Eleanor, and who was the first person?"

"One of the caterers, I think."

"Who else?" For some reason, Lilah felt the need to know.

"I really don't know. I didn't look."

"That other judge? Your boss?"

"I doubt it. He doesn't move that quickly these days with his cane."

"But so many of the people here are from the courthouse." She knew because the groom was an assistant district attorney, the bride an assistant to the mayor, and distantly related by marriage to Ashe's boss, the administrative judge.

"Yes, they are," Ashe said. "It's an incestuous place. Small town. We all know each other. A lot of us date each other or have from time to time."

"Everyone you work with in that building will hear about this by Monday morning, won't they?"

"Sooner, I'd think. The gossip system is highly efficient in our little world," he admitted, looking none too pleased at that.

"I feel terrible about this," she said.

"It's not your fault," he insisted. "I was the one who wanted you stripped bare on the desk...."

Yeah, not the time to think about that.

Him stripping her bare on the desk and *feasting* on her. She shivered at the thought.

He swore softly, then said, "It just never occurred to me to check and see if the lock would hold."

"I'm sure I wouldn't have, either," she admitted.

He looked truly annoyed. "So, I guess it's a good thing we didn't get any farther than we did."

"Yes," she agreed. He'd said this wouldn't be wise. She doubted he ever imagined it turning out this badly. She just wanted to hide, from him and everyone else.

"I'm really sorry," she said again, barely able to look him in the eye.

"Me, too."

"I'm going to stay here and lie low, until more of these people leave," she decided.

He nodded. "And I really should go. It's been a long day. I guess I'll take my chances with whoever's out there, between me and my car."

"Go ahead." And then she had no idea what to say.

"Thank you for listening to me about the case. It helped. But I have to ask you not to tell anyone what I said about it."

"Of course, I won't."

He nodded. "Good night, Lilah."

"Good night."

Eleanor was gleeful the next afternoon. Once all the wedding guests had departed, she had her friends Kathleen and Gladdy over for a late lunch on the terrace to share the good news about Lilah and the judge. It was proving to be ridiculously easy, no challenge at all, after they'd been so worried that Lilah might prove difficult.

They were enjoying their success when Wyatt arrived, kissing cheeks and wanting them to take pity on him and feed him with his wife, Jane, out of town promoting her new book on women's financial independence. Jane had warned them that the poor boy was a dreadful cook, on the rare occasions that he even tried.

"So, ladies, how goes the great plan?" he asked, taking a seat at the patio table.

"You haven't heard?" Kathleen asked. "What did you do last night?"

He shook his head. "I left the wedding reception fairly early to catch a football game on TV, slept in, woke up hungry and came straight here. What would I have heard?"

"Eleanor was simply brilliant yesterday."

"I'm sure she was," Wyatt said, ever the charmer.

"With her matchmaking, dear," Gladdy told him.

"With Ashe? You're actually making progress with him and Lilah? I don't believe it."

"You've never fully appreciated what we do, and I just don't see how that can be, given the fact that you would never even have met Jane, if not for us, and I know you are blissfully happy with her. Show some respect, you rascal," Kathleen told him.

"Sorry. I've been without my wife for too long, and my mood is not the best. When she gets back, I'll be perfectly pleasant to everyone. Please, tell me what you managed to do with Ashe."

They giggled, all three of them.

"No way. It can't have been that good. It's Ashe. He's

completely reformed since he took the bench, no fun at all anymore," Wyatt insisted.

"Eleanor managed to get them alone in the study yesterday as the reception was winding down," Gladdy told him.

"Your friend and Lilah apparently had a very good time in the study last night," Kathleen added.

"A good time? And we know this...how?"

"Because the lock on the study door doesn't work," Eleanor said.

"No way," Wyatt claimed.

"Oh, yes. I'm never getting that lock fixed now. It could come in handy in the future," Eleanor said.

"Have you seen Lilah yet?" Kathleen asked her.

"No, she's hiding, but she'll have to come out of her room sooner or later."

Wyatt gaped at them with a combination of disbelief and amazement. "I was sure he was only doing this because I basically dared him to, and then begged him to, and that Lilah was doing this because she needed him for some wacky-sounding thing. What was it?"

"Her divorce ceremony," Eleanor said. "I'm not even sure if he's actually agreed to do it. Lilah hasn't gotten to the point in her classes where the divorce ceremony comes in yet. It's near the end, I'm sure."

"Ladies, I'm truly in awe of you all," Wyatt admitted.

"I told you," Kathleen said. "You've never fully appreciated how good we are at this."

Ashe reported directly to Judge Walters's chambers, as ordered, first thing Monday morning.

"At my ex-wife's niece's wedding?" the old man railed from behind his messy desk. "You just had to carry on like that at her wedding?"

Reception, actually, but Ashe wasn't going to argue that. He knew the drill with Judge Walters. Stand at attention and say as little as possible. "I'm very sorry, sir."

"Thank the Lord that Dana and my daughter both had the good sense not to marry you. I still can't believe that girl...what was her name?"

"Regina Brower," he supplied.

"Yes, her. I can't believe she ever married you, although I'll give her the benefit of the doubt, being so ridiculously young when she did it."

"Yes, sir." Ashe had been only twenty-one himself, blinded by her beauty, her skills in bed, her highly respectable family name and the mind-numbingly crazy workload of a first-year law student.

"You know, I never liked you—"

"I'm very much aware of that, sir—"

"But I never thought you were an idiot. Do I really need to tell you that this sort of thing is not what you want voters to know about you?"

"No, sir."

"And if anyone got photos or—God help us—video, it will show up on the internet just like that." Judge Walters snapped his fingers. "And you'll be through. Judges do not engage in sexual behavior in public!"

"Yes, sir." He was fairly certain there were no photos, and even if there were, at worst he thought they might show his back and a bit of Lilah's skirt. He thought he'd blocked everyone's view pretty well.

Okay, he forgot, her turquoise top lying on the floor and that little bit of a bra she wore. Something he'd found insanely sexy when he'd picked it up and handed it to her, especially when she'd put it back on and he'd realized just how little there was to it and why her breasts seemed so... free...and moved the way they did beneath her clothes.

Ashe swore silently to himself. *Not the time.*

"And here I was starting to think you were actually worth something on the bench. That we might want to keep you around," Judge Walters said.

High praise from him, where Ashe was concerned.

"That woman looks like nothing but trouble, and I would have thought you could spot one of those a mile away, son," the judge said.

"Yes, sir." He'd known she was trouble right away and done it anyway. What the hell had happened to him? He couldn't understand it.

"All right. That's it. Get out of here. And don't give me reason to call you back in here," the judge ordered.

Ashe hurried to the door, not wanting to give the man time to come up with any other grievances against him.

Walking through the courthouse, he could feel people's gazes following his every move, hear the whispers. Someone had taped one of Lilah's posters for her class to the outer door of his chambers. He yanked it down and crumpled it up as he went inside.

His clerk, Mrs. Davis, a '50s-era, schoolmarmish type of woman, was on the phone as he entered the office. She looked as if she'd swallowed her own tongue, she shut up so fast, as he passed her with a nod and a quick, "Morning."

"Morning, Judge," she practically squeaked, as he kept on moving. "Your friend Mr. Gray is waiting in your chambers."

Perfect, Ashe thought, opening the door to his private chambers and finding Wyatt lounging comfortably, grinning from ear to ear. Ashe closed the door, tossed Lilah's advertisement in the trash can and sat down behind his desk.

"So," Wyatt asked, "were you really naked?"

"No! I had all of my clothes on."

"Was she naked?"

"No. She most definitely had...the vast majority of her clothes on," he claimed, reasoning that the skirts she preferred were long and full and flowing. Tons of material there, so much more than there'd been to her top or that tiny bra. So what he'd said was technically correct.

"Really?" Wyatt said. "Because Eleanor took pity on me and fed me yesterday, and she seemed awfully happy about what went on in the study...."

"Yeah. That woman is up to something—"

"I told you. They always are. All of them—"

"And Jane's aunt? Gladdy?"

"Great aunt," Wyatt said.

"Have you ever wondered if she was in the early stages of Alzheimer's? Because with that, people tend to lose... their inhibitions...."

"Inhibitions? Honestly, I don't think she ever had any. Kathleen, either. The stories Jane's told me, and Gladdy herself... She and Kathleen have definitely lived life to the fullest," Wyatt said. "Why? Did she flirt with you?"

He remembered their thorough assessment of his physique. "Yes."

"She does that. She likes men. Kathleen, too. There was a time when Jane and I thought they were going to come to blows over my uncle, before he died."

Ashe just looked at him, trying to figure out if he was morally obligated to say more, if the poor woman truly needed medical help or was just naturally outrageous and inappropriate.

"Gladdy didn't really do anything, did she?" Wyatt asked.

"No, she didn't."

"Didn't think so. You're just trying to change the subject. Which is, you and Lilah in the study during Judge Walters's ex-wife's niece's wedding?" Wyatt laughed out loud. "God, what were you thinking?"

"I wasn't," Ashe admitted, still baffled by the whole thing. "Obviously. If you're going to lock a door for a reason, make damned sure the lock works."

"But I thought you didn't even like her?"

"I didn't. I was almost sure I didn't," Ashe said.

"Naked with you at Malone's, naked on that poster—"

"She was not naked at Malone's, and she's not the naked woman on the poster—"

"And now naked with you in the study. People are just calling her the Naked Woman. No name. Just the Naked Woman. Every man's dream."

"Not mine," Ashe insisted.

"Oh, please. You're not any kind of a saint. You like a naked woman as much as the rest of us, you just like yours in complete privacy."

"Well, yeah. Public nudity is where this whole thing started—"

"Wait, what?" Wyatt jumped right on that. "You swore no one was naked in public."

"Yeah. No." Ashe hardly even knew what he was saying. "Lilah wasn't. No one was. It doesn't matter. I knew this was a bad idea all along. And you're the one who got me into this."

"I said it would be a good thing for you to get to know Eleanor."

"Not like this! Not by fooling around with her cousin in her study during a wedding reception at her estate."

"Yeah, well, I never thought you'd do that," Wyatt explained. "I'm proud of you. You're not as dull as I thought since you took your seat on the bench."

"This is not helping," Ashe said.

Wyatt laughed deep in his chest.

"You know," Ashe threatened, "I could call the bailiff and have you thrown into a cell on nothing but my say-so."

Wyatt grinned. "The locks work there?"

## Chapter Six

It was embarrassing and childish, but Lilah hid like a coward for the rest of Saturday and all day Sunday, unwilling to face Eleanor and her friends. Monday came, and she managed to slip out of the house without seeing anyone, heading for town to run errands.

She had an idea for helping that poor teenager with cancer Ashe had told her about, Wendy Marx. Lilah had found her name in the newspaper story. Lilah shot her own publicity photos for her classes. Photography was a hobby. She might not be able to make Wendy look pretty every day, but she could make her gorgeous in a photo, and maybe that would make Wendy happy.

Lilah was excited about that part of her errands, not so much about her need to get a business license. That meant a trip to the courthouse where Ashe worked. She did absolutely everything else on her list first, and then, when there was nothing left, walked down the block from the bank and stood in front of the courthouse.

*Coward,* she called herself. Although that was the word that had gotten her into the study to face Ashe, and look how that had turned out.

She could go in there, get her business license and not see him, she thought. Surely there were all sorts of functions housed in the courthouse, lots of people coming and going. She marched inside, found a directory sending her to the second floor, noted courtrooms were on the third. She stood waiting for the elevator, thinking she was safe. Then the doors opened, and there was Ashe.

He saw her and froze, as if he couldn't quite believe what he was seeing, obviously not happy to find her here. People started getting off the elevator, and he just stood there. So finally, Lilah got on.

"What are you doing here?" he asked in a hushed voice.

"I need a business license." She stood beside him in the back of the elevator, noting that at least two of the other four people in the elevator kept looking back at her and Ashe. One seemed to be giggling very softly.

Ashe gave a little growl of annoyance.

"I'm sorry. I thought I could get in and out without seeing you," she told him. "Although I did wonder if people know about what happened and are giving you a hard time."

And with that, the giggling woman in front of them leaned in close to another woman standing beside her and began whispering ever-so-quietly in the other woman's ear.

*Okay,* people knew.

And were enjoying it, judging by the way the other woman now had a hand clamped firmly over her mouth, struggling not to make a sound, as she darted furtive glances back at Ashe and Lilah.

The elevator got to the second floor, and Lilah went

to get off, but Ashe stopped her, still holding on to her arm. When she looked up at him, he just shook his head no. So they rode to the third floor, and then he led her down a nearly deserted hallway, through a door that had his name on it, through an inner office and then into what could only be the judge's chambers.

He closed the door firmly behind them and then waited there, a puzzled look on his face as he turned and stared at the door.

"What?" she asked.

"This door actually locks, and I'm trying to figure out if it would be better if no one could get in here to find us together. Or worse, if they knew we were in here together behind a locked door. I honestly don't know."

Lilah suspected he seldom found himself in situations where he would hesitate over something as simple as whether or not to lock a door.

"I…I can just go," she offered. "I didn't realize it was that bad, me simply walking into the same building where you work."

He was still trying to figure out the door. He opened it wide for a moment, thought about it some more. She expected him to close it back, but he didn't. He left it open maybe six inches, so that they weren't behind a closed or locked door, but no one would just glance through the doorway and see them. It seemed important to him to get the door thing exactly right.

Finally, he motioned for her to take a seat in front of his desk, and then he put himself on the other side of it, standing there leaning against the credenza behind him and staring at her again.

"What?" she asked finally.

"I have no idea what to say to you," he finally admitted.

"And that's…awful?" Because he looked as if it felt awful.

"I hate not knowing what to do."

"Me, too," she agreed. "Although, I'm not even sure what we're talking about. Whether you should sneak me out of the building now, before anyone else sees me with you right now? Or whether you should ever see me again?"

"Both," he said.

*Both?* Okay.

"It would help if there wasn't a desk between us," he said flatly. "Although, having one between us is better than having you on it and me on top of you."

"Oh, that." She hadn't imagined that, after the incident in the study, being anywhere in the vicinity of a desk with her would be a problem for him. Or her, actually. Now that she looked at it, thought about it… His desk was ridiculously neat, practically bare—

*Oops,* not a good word right now.

She'd dreamed about him and her on the desk, her on it and him on top of her, as he'd so bluntly put it. Just hearing the words had turned her on.

"Yeah, thinking of us on the desk is a problem," he said. "Having one handy right now is a problem. You, here in my chambers with me and my desk, is a problem—"

"So, now, basically, I'm a problem?" she shot back at him, going from turned on to annoyed in three seconds flat.

"I was sure of that from the first moment I saw you," he claimed.

"Well, I don't have to be your problem—"

At some point, she stood up to go, but before she could, he was around the side of the desk and had his hands on her, holding her in front of him, just far enough away that their bodies weren't touching.

"I didn't mean it like that." He leaned in close, still just shy of touching her anywhere but her arms. But she felt the heat coming off his body, felt that little zing of awareness zipping through her. "Me, thinking of you on the desk, is a problem. Me, wanting you on any convenient, horizontal surface, is a problem.

"Oh." She got it then. And she'd never been devoured on a desk before. Finally, she whispered. "I've...been thinking about it, too."

At which point, he swore softly, repeatedly, and lowered his forehead to rest against hers. "Lilah, please..."

"Please, what?"

"That is not helping," he complained. "Help me figure this out. I just can't seem to think or be sensible around you."

"I don't want to cause any more trouble for you," she said, because honestly and truly she didn't. "But I like the idea of leaving you unable to think or be sensible."

He swore once again and then leaned down and kissed her, his mouth hard and insistent and even a bit impatient, which was another little thrill for her, after the extreme patience he'd shown that night in the study.

When he lifted his mouth, she asked, "Are you really always sensible?"

"For years now," he said. "Cautious, too."

"Why?"

"Because I wasn't always when I was younger. I come from a family of people who definitely were not sensible or cautious. My father was a crook who scammed a bunch of people in this town out of their money. He went to prison when I was ten. My mother started drinking and never stopped. So being cautious, careful, being someone people respect means something to me. I didn't like the life I had back then, so I changed it."

"Oh." She understood and admired that. She'd most definitely been unhappy with her life and worked hard to change it.

"We should talk about this. About us. Just talk," he said. "Not here."

She nodded.

"My house," he said. "I live alone. It's private...." He looked troubled. "Maybe too private. Maybe we shouldn't be alone until we know...what we're going to do. Yeah, that's probably smart. So, not here. Not at Eleanor's. Someplace private but not too private. I'll think of a place. What are you doing tonight?"

"I'm teaching tonight, but my class will be over at eight-thirty or so."

"Your class?" That seemed to worry him.

"Don't say you won't help me with it. Not yet. It's weeks before we'll get to the point where we're ready for the divorce ceremony. Just don't say no yet."

"Fine. Not yet. I'll call you with a place where we can meet tonight."

She nodded, then just stood there, looking at him. He confused her, too, and excited her and flat-out turned her on. Or was it just that he was the first man she'd been attracted to since her marriage had ended? Lilah honestly wasn't sure. She didn't trust herself all that much at the moment to know what she wanted or why she wanted it. So it was good that she'd have some time to think, and then they would talk.

"I should go," she said.

He nodded but didn't move, just gave her a smoldering look.

It seemed he didn't want her to go any more than she

wanted to leave. And it was a heady feeling, knowing she made him feel this way, too.

He swore softly, she grinned and then he was kissing her again, devouring her, and it was every bit as glorious as it had been Saturday night. He moved with a calm insistence and thoroughness that was maddening and yet so very sexy. A part of her wanted to grab him and take control, push him to move faster and faster, and a part of her wanted to just go limp against him, letting him do whatever he wanted because it felt so good.

He was holding her close, and she could feel the edge of his desk behind her. He muttered against her mouth, "Don't you dare get on that desk."

"Why not?" she asked.

"You know exactly why not."

She laughed, a sound caught by his mouth, that wickedly talented mouth of his, and she thought she absolutely loved the taste of him, the heat of his body against hers.

"And do not let me take a stitch of clothing off you," he told her, as one of his big, warm hands moved to cup her breast.

"All right. I won't," she promised.

"Are you wearing that tiny little scrap of a bra you had on the other night?"

"One just like it except peach-colored."

He groaned, rubbed his thumb across her nipple and started nibbling on her neck. She had her hands in his hair, holding his head down to hers, and in her imagination, she couldn't see anything except herself stretched out on a big, bare desktop, him slowly and deliberately uncovering every inch of her, exploring her body at leisure.

But that wasn't going to happen. Not here, not now. She didn't want to cause trouble for him, because if she did, she might never get this close to him again, and Lilah liked being close to him.

So she kissed him back, rubbing her body up against his until he swore and tore his mouth from hers. "Stop that."

"Do I have to?"

"Yes, you do."

But he was still kissing her.

"Maybe I could come back, after everyone else is gone. Your desk is so big and neat and clean, and I've never been ravaged on a desk before—"

He groaned, took her firmly and pushed her away, holding her at arm's length, his eyes blazing down into hers. He was breathing hard, frowning, tense.

"Too much?" she guessed.

"You cannot make me think about that in here. I have to work in this office, at this desk. It's already hard enough to do that, Lilah—"

And then he went still and quiet, listening.

She thought she heard someone come into the outer office, two women talking. He gave her a quick assessing look. She could only imagine what he saw. True, she had all her clothes on, and she'd never gotten up on the desk. But her mouth felt full and tingly, having been thoroughly kissed. Her breath wasn't steady, either, and it was almost as if she could still feel his hand on her breast; her nipples puckered up against the fabric of her clothes.

He pointed to a door off to the side and then touched his finger to his lips, asking her to be quiet. She walked as softly as possible to the door, and he followed her, reaching around her to open it. She walked through and found herself in a courtroom.

Lilah laughed softly, then turned to him. "I thought you were trying to get me to hide in your closet."

He laughed, too, reaching for her again.

And then, she realized someone else was laughing, as well.

A woman and a man, sitting in the empty courtroom looking over some files on the table in front of them, the woman looking vaguely familiar.

Ashe's hand fell away from her side, and he looked grim.

"Your Honor," the woman said, managing to sound both deferential and mischievous at the same time. "My client and I were just looking for a quiet space before court resumes this afternoon. All the meeting rooms were full, and I didn't realize you'd be...using the courtroom."

"We're not," he said.

"We can leave," the woman offered, getting to her feet, the man beside her rising to his feet, too.

"No, it's fine. We're just passing through," Ashe insisted.

"You were at the wedding," Lilah said, only then figuring it out. "In the wedding, actually, right?"

The woman nodded and held out her hand to Lilah. "Allison Walters. The bride is a good friend, and my great uncle is the administrative judge here."

"Allie, this is Lilah Ryan, a cousin of Eleanor Barrington Holmes," Ashe said tightly.

Allison Walters shook Lilah's hand, looking delighted. "The estate was absolutely beautiful. I'm so glad Dana chose it for her wedding. Everything worked perfectly.... Well, except for one little thing, I heard."

"Oh?" Lilah asked.

"Let's go, Lilah," Ashe said, hustling her out of there before she could say anything else.

"But, if the bride was unhappy, I'm sure Eleanor would

like to know about it. I was just going to ask what didn't work—"

"The lock on the study door," Ashe told Lilah. "That's what Allie was talking about."

"Oh." *That*. "And her uncle is—"

"My boss. I told you it was an incestuous world at the courthouse."

"I made things worse, didn't I?" Lilah asked.

"I think we both did that," he said, steering her to the elevator and then pushing the button to summon it.

"Well...I'll just be going then. Sorry," she said, as the elevator doors opened and she walked inside.

Ashe stood there staring at her, and she couldn't help but think of how perfect the man looked, how serious and strong and respectable. She thought again of the heady knowledge that she could make him a little bit crazy and of how good it felt to kiss him.

"I'll call you about tonight," he said.

And then, right before the elevator doors closed, she noticed—too late to tell him—that he had a little bit of her lipstick on his otherwise perfect cheek.

It was a full fifteen minutes later, after he'd walked downstairs to the tiny cafeteria for a sandwich and was headed back to his office, amidst numerous odd looks from the people he passed, that he finally figured out what was going on.

He ran into Wyatt, who practically laughed in his face and then steered him into the men's room and in front of the big mirror there.

Ashe had lipstick on his cheek.

A lip-shaped impression in the soft pink that was so close to the natural color of Lilah's lips, he hadn't thought she was wearing lipstick. He certainly hadn't thought to check if she'd left a mark on him.

"Hey, at least you both had your clothes on this time," Wyatt said, laughing. "Or so I heard. Fully clothed, right?"

Ashe wiped the telltale mark off his cheek and glared at Wyatt.

"And in your own courtroom. That's much more daring than I imagined you'd be—"

"We were not doing anything in the courtroom, except walking through it—"

"Oh. Had her in the office, huh? That's still—"

"No, I did not *have* her in the office," Ashe said a bit too loudly, especially when he realized someone had just walked into the bathroom. A clerk in another judge's court, he realized. *Perfect.* "The woman is a walking disaster to me. Every time I see her, something goes wrong."

Wyatt laughed again. "Then stop seeing her."

Right, like he could do *that*.

"Wait, you want to see her." Wyatt pounced on the idea. "You really want to see her. How about that?"

"She's...she's..." Ashe stumbled over his words, thinking about a half dozen things she was—maddening, confusing and so sexy.

"Look at you. You're a mess over this woman. I love it!" Wyatt said.

"I am not. I'm just... It's been a while, okay? Cynthia moved... Has it already been six months ago? And I've been really busy with work, just haven't gotten out much and met anybody new. That's all," Ashe reasoned.

"Right. Busy. I'm sure that's all it is."

But he didn't say it like that. He said it like, *I don't believe that's all it is any more than you do.*

"You should do something about that," Wyatt said, ever helpful.

"I will."

He'd get Lilah in his house, behind many locked doors, all of which worked, with absolutely no one else anywhere in the house, no one to walk in on them, no one to gossip about them. Then he was going to take her to bed or to any convenient, flat surface he could find and get her out of his system.

That's what he was going to do.

No problem.

Lilah walked in something of a daze through the down town streets toward where she'd parked her car, her body still hot and all tingly after her encounter with Ashe. She was nervous but excited, too, unable to stop thinking of seeing him that evening and what might happen then.

She wasn't sure what he expected, what he wanted... Okay, she knew one thing she was pretty sure he wanted—her naked—and yes, a part of her wanted that too. Very much.

But a part of her remembered that she'd just gotten out of a marriage that ended badly, and that she'd never been the kind of woman who jumped into bed with men casually or even quickly.

Not that anything with Ashe felt casual, just fast. Gloriously fast and exciting and freeing and maybe even healing to a woman who hadn't felt truly desired and desirable in a long time.

She deserved to feel that way, didn't she?

Both desirable and desired?

And he was such a sexy man. She absolutely loved feeling that she could make him lose control completely.

How many women did that to him? She really wanted

to believe not a lot, mostly because he seemed so in control in every other instance she'd witnessed so far.

And he made her want to be outrageous and free and simply enjoy every moment she could have with him.

He'd made her walk out of the courthouse without so much as a second thought about the reason she'd gone there in the first place—her business license. And now had her walking aimlessly through downtown.

She passed the bakery that Eleanor's godson's wife, Amy, owned and stopped in to say hello and buy a couple of fresh croissants. She passed the restaurant where she'd had lunch with Ashe, the bank where she'd opened an account and then…a lingerie store.

Lilah walked past it the first time and then turned and looked around, wondering if there could possibly be anyone on the street at that moment who knew her or knew Ashe. They really had the worst luck. It seemed as if every time he touched her, someone caught them.

But it would be nice to have something really pretty and sexy to wear for him that evening. Oh, he liked her little bras, and she was happy about that. But she wore them because they were comfortable, mostly, and besides, he'd seen them.

She lingered in front of the health food store next door, and when foot traffic on the street came to a minimum, Lilah hurried into the lingerie store. Immediately she headed to the back, away from the windows facing the street, barely giving the woman behind the counter time to greet her.

There she found herself in the midst of all sorts of pretty colors, satins, silks, laces of all kinds, from elegant nightgowns to outrageously sexy underwear. She didn't know where to start. It had been a long time since she'd bought things solely with an eye toward pleasing a man and turning him on.

*What would Ashe like?*

He liked her bras, so she was thinking…delicate, pretty-sexy was likely his thing, and there were plenty of things that qualified as pretty-sexy in the store.

She finally settled on a flesh-colored mini slip. It had thin silk straps, like an old-fashioned full slip, but then it turned into an abbreviated, stretchy, clingy, lacy thing, with a scooped-out neckline, that cupped her breasts and hugged her waist before flaring ever so slightly at the hips, barely—just barely—covering her bottom. It was completely sheer in some places, not quite sheer in others.

Lilah got all hot and bothered all over again just trying it on, imagining the heat flaring in Ashe's eyes when he saw her in it. Honestly, she wasn't sure she had the nerve to wear it for him.

"Is it a slip?" Lilah asked the elegant woman at the register. "Or a nightgown? Or something else?"

The woman smiled knowingly. "It's whatever you want it to be."

"Oh. Okay."

Lilah wasn't sure what she wanted it to be, but she bought it.

The woman introduced herself as Sybil Gardner, the owner of the boutique, then said, "I believe you're the woman behind that beautiful poster for the divorce classes that's hanging in my window?"

"Yes, that's me," Lilah said.

"We should talk. All those women starting over…they need to feel beautiful. Nothing makes a woman feel beautiful like beautiful underthings. Nothing except a man to admire her in them and then take them off of her."

Lilah just nodded.

"Those women attending your class? You should take them on a field trip to my store."

Eleanor nearly squealed with delight when she saw Lilah walk in with one of those distinctive black bags with the big, white scripted S. She hurried back to Kathleen and Gladdy, who were sitting on the back patio and said, "Lilah went to Sybil's!"

They oohed and ahhed, grinning.

"When?" Kathleen asked.

"She just walked in with a bag from there."

"I was afraid, after what she went through with that terrible ex-husband of hers, she'd be gun-shy about men. But the judge is obviously too delicious a man to resist."

"I wouldn't think of resisting him," Gladdy said.

"Me, either," Kathleen added. "This is all going perfectly. We're brilliant, ladies. Just brilliant."

## Chapter Seven

Ashe was a mess but managed to get through the rest of the day without incident. He made himself stay late and try to catch up on his reading, waiting for Lilah to finish her class, thinking of all the reasons he should not bring her back to his house.

One, he didn't normally bring women there. It was his house, after all. Two, and more importantly, it was completely private—too private. No one would walk in on them, and even if someone tried, all the locks on all the doors worked, and he had a great security system. Ashe knew this. He was a judge. He had to be careful. Three, he had a desk there, a big, solid desk where he worked and had to be able to concentrate, not think of what he'd done to Lilah on top of it. Home was out, he decided quite rationally.

He just needed a place where no one would see them but he wouldn't be tempted to ravish the woman the moment he saw her—not an easy combination to find. A restaurant was likely his best bet. An out-of-the-way, fairly dark, quiet restaurant where no one in the legal community ever went. But how was he supposed to know of the place if he never went there?

He ended up at the Barrington estate a full half hour early, impossibly eager as he got out of his car and heard Lilah's voice. Following the sound, rounding the back, left corner of the house, he found her on the patio, sitting in a circle with ten other women. It appeared they'd done some sort of art project. If he had to guess, he'd say finger painting. Did grown women finger paint?

They'd scribbled all over their drawings, things he couldn't make out. One of the women was holding up her drawing and talking, and the others were listening. Many of them either were currently in tears or had red-rimmed eyes and tissues in hand.

Ashe planned to make a hasty retreat, but Lilah looked up and saw him, told him they were done with their art projects and asked him to stay. He ended up giving her class a quick explanation of divorce law in Maryland and answering a few questions they had before the class broke up.

Together, they waited for Lilah's class to leave, and then she led him into the kitchen, where she said, "Thank you for that."

"No problem."

"Can I maybe get one more favor?"

"Name it." He'd do just about anything for her right now, especially if it meant he'd have her in his arms soon.

"Remember when I told you I sometimes end up with women in my classes who are being abused? Well, I've got one—"

"Don't tell me her name. I don't want to know. She might end up in my courtroom one day."

"Okay."

"And I really wish you wouldn't have anything to do with this. I told you, it's one of the most volatile situations on the planet."

"Ashe, just give me a name, please. A police officer who'll take this seriously. You know some of them are much better than others with this sort of thing."

He didn't like this. Not at all. But she was right. Some cops were much better at it than others.

"Please?" she asked, like a woman who had him wrapped around her little finger. *Damn.*

"Dan Brewer," he said finally. "I don't have his number, but call the police department's main line, and they'll find him for you."

"Thank you."

"Be careful. Promise me."

"I will," she said, grinning sweetly. "I was surprised to see you here. I thought you were going to call me and tell me where to meet you."

"I was," he said, surprised by his own impatience. He hadn't been able to wait. Scary thought, there. "Then thought I might as well pick you up."

It was what a gentleman did, after all. He tried to be gentleman.

Although mostly he was thinking what he really wanted to do was kiss her, right now. She looked so.. alive. Her skirt was a bold scarlet and black, like a flame reaching nearly to the floor. Her bare feet poked out beneath it, toes painted a matching scarlet. Her top was white and simple, dipping low along her neckline, the sleeves—were those tiny sleeves?—sliding slightly down her shoulders and arms, leaving a sweeping stretch of bare skin along her neck and shoulders.

"I want to nibble on you," he said, almost without realizing he'd actually let the words out.

She smiled broadly.

"Not here," he said. "But I don't want to have to wait long to do it."

Lilah took him by the hand and led him down the hall toward the side door, but turned left instead through another door. He found himself in a bedroom.

"Maid's quarters," she said. "Eleanor offered me my pick of bedrooms upstairs, but she uses them as guest rooms during events, and I didn't want to take up one of those. Plus, this was the most private room in the house. And the lock works. I checked after we got caught in the study. You know…just in case."

Just in case he wanted to ravish her in the house?

*Bad, bad, bad idea.*

He just had to kiss her, that was all.

Could he do that and only that?

He gave it a shot, taking her by the arms and backing her up to the wall, his body pinning her there, taking a moment to stare down into her eyes before he let himself have the first taste of her.

Her arms slipped beneath his jacket and around him, holding him to her. "You changed your mind. You said we should talk. Nothing but talk."

"Yes, I changed my mind. Is that all right with you?"

She nodded.

"I'm going to kiss you. Not for long. And then we're getting out of here and going somewhere. To talk."

"Okay," she said, as if he could have suggested jumping off a cliff and flying, and she'd have been perfectly agreeable.

"You are a dangerous woman," he said.

She licked her lips and smiled, and that was it.

He couldn't take it anymore.

He was kissing her like crazy, hot, sizzling, deep, no-holds-barred kissing. He wanted his hands all over her, wanted her naked. The wall would do just fine for the moment. He could hold her there with his body, get up under that flame-colored skirt. No need to take the time to strip it off of her. If she'd wrap her legs around his waist and hang on to him, they'd be fine. He was nearly blind to everything but that image—of him and her up against the wall of a room in Eleanor's house.

He backed off, breathing hard, begging silently for strength, and she just stood there, looking at him and smiling, an open invitation it seemed.

"We really shouldn't do this here," he said with what might have been his last shred of sanity.

"I know," she said.

"It would help if you didn't look quite so willing."

"You want me to look like I don't want you?"

"It would help," he repeated.

She took a breath. "I'm not sure if I can. Maybe you could just…stop looking at me?"

"No way," he told her.

"Then I guess we have a problem." But she was grinning. Obviously, she liked the problem.

"We should go. Now," he said. "My house is ten minutes away. I'll get us there in five. Small town. The cops know all the judges' cars. No one's going to pull me over."

"Okay," she said, then, "Wait. I got something for you."

She went to the bed and grabbed a distinctive, glossy black-and-white shopping bag.

Ashe swore. "You went to Sybil's today?"

She nodded. "You know the place?"

He nodded. Every man in town recognized that black-and-white bag with the big S on it. If a man was lucky, he had a woman he shopped for there on Christmas, New Year's, birthdays.

Lilah in her flame-red skirt, leaving him at the court-house with lipstick on his cheek and heading to Sybil's…

Not exactly the kind of discretion he was hoping for.

"What?" she asked. "You'll like it. Although, I have to admit, I'm not really sure what it is. I was thinking a slip, but maybe it's not. People really don't make full slips anymore. Not that it's all that full. Or long. But I think it will work, and it was pretty."

She reached into the bag and pulled out a mostly see-through, flesh-colored thing and held it up in front of her-self.

"What do you think?" she asked, either pure innocence or pure vixen. He honestly couldn't tell.

He groaned, swore once again, and then tried to look away, but couldn't.

*Put it on,* he thought. *Put it on and nothing else, and then stand over here against the wall.*

They could do this right now. It would be over in about sixty seconds flat, but who cared? They could do it all over again, more slowly the next time.

"Ashe, what's wrong?" she asked.

"Please, put that away," he begged.

"You don't like it?"

"I like it. I like it a lot. Do you want to do this right here, right now? With three nosy women here, maybe listening in from the kitchen?"

"No," she said.

"Then put it away."

"Well, should I put it on under my clothes?"

"God, no—"

"Take it with us?" she tried again.

He whimpered. Actually whimpered like a little kid. It was just too much. He was picturing her in that thing now, that tiny scrap of a thing and only that, all bare legs and sheer lace. He was going insane.

"What do you want me to do, Ashe?" she asked.

"I got it." He took the slip thing from her, treating it like something that might scald his skin at the very touch, crumpled it up to almost nothing and shoved it into his pocket. "Do you need anything else?"

She shook her head.

"Great." He took her by the hand. "Let's go."

He got her out of the building without running into anyone, got her into his car and to his house in the five minutes he promised, then wondered if she'd be offended if he grabbed her the second he closed and locked the front door behind them.

Maybe, he decided.

He didn't want to blow this now.

She'd started chattering on the way over, and he thought she was a little bit nervous, plus he had that tiny lace thing she'd bought for him balled up in his pocket. Could he stand to give her time to put it on? Could he stand seeing her in it? Maybe not the first time, he decided. They had all night. At least he hoped they did.

What were his options here? Bedroom, sofa, his desk… It was difficult to decide, as if his brain had been invaded by a pesky, cumbersome fog that clouded his thinking. He was only half following what she was saying.

*Florida.*

*House on the market.*

*Trouble selling it.*

*At loose ends with her job.*

*Wanting a change.*

*Trying out being in Maryland again.*

*Waiting for her divorce to be final...*

He'd backed her against the wall, thinking it was the closest space and it would work, and she was driving him crazy, and it had obviously been too long since he'd been with any woman. He had started out nuzzling her jaw and then nibbling on her neck while she kept chattering.

Nerves, he thought.

The woman talked when she was nervous.

He'd help her forget all about being nervous.

But the words *waiting* and *divorce* got through even the fog in his sex-crazed brain. His head popped up. No more neck-nibbling for him, not right now.

"Wait," he said, staring down at her. "You are divorced, aren't you?"

She gave him a blank look.

Had she already moved on to a different topic, and had it taken him a moment to process, so that he was behind on the conversation? Was that what was wrong?

"Yes," she said.

"For how long?"

"It took forever. Filing paperwork, waiting periods after filing paperwork, time to respond to paperwork, scheduling meetings, finally working out a settlement agreement and then more filing of paperwork, then waiting for a hearing. I thought it would never be over," she explained.

Maybe he wasn't making himself clear. Maybe he couldn't, because he could hardly think. But his mind was stuck on this one point. "Okay, but the actual divorce decree has been issued?"

"Well, I haven't gotten the actual decree in the mail yet. I'm still waiting—"

He let go of her as if she was made of boiling water capable of scalding him if he let his hands stay on her another second, then stood there, stunned. How did he not know this? How had he not asked?

*Oh, this was bad. So very bad.*

"You're not divorced," he said.

"No, we signed everything. We agreed. We went to court. The judge granted the petition. I'm divorced."

"When?" he insisted.

"Right before I came here."

He groaned. "When was that? A month ago?"

"Not...not quite," she admitted. "Why?"

"Because there's a waiting period. The judge signs the order, but it's not final for some period of time. A month? Two? I don't know. It's different in every state, but most of them have waiting periods. At the end of the waiting period, you're divorced. Not before."

She frowned. "Are you sure?"

He nodded. Give him his laptop and a minute to search he'd quote Florida law word-for-word to her, if that's what it took.

"But...I...I thought I was divorced. I feel divorced. I had my own little divorce ceremony. I even burned a few things—"

"Burned things?" *What did she burn?*

"Just a little ritual to mark the occasion. Or what I thought was the occasion!" She looked so mad. "I was so glad it was over. I was sure it was, and I certainly wanted it to be. Not to mention that my ex-husband has been acting like he was divorced for a couple of years now.... That should count for something!"

He nodded, his head practically spinning. "Exactly how long have you been here?"

"Almost a month," she said. "So, I could actually be

divorced already and just not know it yet, because the paperwork is in the mail, right?"

"Maybe," he agreed.

She seemed puzzled. "This really matters to you?"

He nodded.

"Really?"

"Yes. I don't get involved with married women."

"But I might not be. And even if I still am… My ex walked out on me a year ago, when I found out he was seeing someone else, and he'd been sleeping with her for a while before that. So it isn't like I've really had a husband for a while…"

"Legally, you have," he said. "Lilah, I'm a judge in family court facing an election. I can't be involved with a married woman."

"So…I should call you when I have the paper in my hand or something?" she asked, obviously furious. "Is that the procedure with you? Leave the paperwork on the nightstand and climb into the bed?"

"I don't have a procedure—" he began.

She laughed. "I'm surprised. You're normally so careful."

"Yes, normally, I am." She'd said it as if it was a bad thing. How could it be a bad thing? "I'm sorry, I don't know what I was thinking. I mean, obviously, I wasn't. This is not a conversation I skip, and I guess…somehow I got the impression it had been a while since your divorce was final, and I never actually asked."

"See, this is where a set procedure could help. Or maybe a checklist. A questionnaire. Fill this out, and if you get all the answers right, you can come home with me. How about that?" she said, then turned and marched toward the front door.

"Lilah, wait." He went after her.

She got out the door to his car and just stared at it in disgust. Then she turned and did the same to him. There were tears rolling down her cheeks, and she was furiously wiping them away.

"I'm sorry," he said. "Really, I am."

Then she started walking down the driveway toward the road.

"Lilah, I'll take you home," he said.

"No, thank you. I can get there myself." She kept on walking.

"There are no sidewalks out here," he pointed out. "There's the road and a drainage ditch on one side."

Damned, stubborn woman, he thought, watching her as she just kept going. At this point, he figured practically everyone in town knew who she was. She was hard to miss in that flame-colored hippie-girl skirt, a woman infamous for the posters up all over town. And if this wouldn't look like a lovers' quarrel, he didn't know what would. Despite all that, he got into his car and drove off after her, slowing as he reached the spot where she was and creeping along in the car beside her.

He had a long driveway, and she hadn't reached the road yet. With luck, he'd get her back in the car before anyone saw her.

"Lilah, please," he said.

She turned and glared at him. "It's really about paperwork and the matter of a few days? If I'd gotten that stupid piece of paper yesterday, everything would be fine? Is that what you're telling me?"

"No—"

"No? Really? Even then, it would be no?"

"It's more than that."

She had stopped walking at one point, but now she'd started again, and he eased the car forward to keep up with her. He feared he saw one of his neighbors—a regular jogger—heading this way, but he couldn't be sure. *Perfect. Just perfect.* He hoped it wasn't the young trophy wife who'd just married the attorney who lived down the road.

"Lilah, just get in the car, please?"

She had pulled ahead of him a little and turned to look back. "Not even if I had the stupid paper? Why? What would be the problem then?"

"You just got divorced. If you're actually divorced at all. It does things to people. It's a lot to process, and you've barely begun to process it now—"

Her mouth fell open, tears still falling down her cheeks. "I've done nothing but work through this process for a year now. A long, frustrating, miserable year. Not to mention the difficulty of the past few years when we were actually married."

"I'm sorry—"

"I twisted myself into knots for that man, trying to make him happy. He wanted to be a college president, and I took a job as the administrative assistant at the student counseling center while I worked on my master's in counseling on the side. I had a ton of different administrative positions on campuses where he worked, following him from place to place, trying to do all the things a good little faculty wife did, and you know my biggest sin? Succeeding faster than he did."

"Yeah, I get that. It's not an uncommon story, I'm sorry to say," Ashe said.

"So when I say, I'm thrilled that the marriage is finally over, I mean I am absolutely, positively thrilled. I felt like cheering when I walked out of that courtroom for the last time. The past few years felt like some kind of brutal survival test, but I did it. I survived, and now, it's done. I don't care what you and your timetable have to say about it. I'm sick of feeling this way, this awful, and I'm ready to start living again."

"Yes, I understand that—"

"So, what's the problem? You don't think I've processed this enough? You have no idea how hard I've worked to process all this crap! I feel like I've run marathons of processing, climbed mountains made of processing!"

"Good for you. I'm glad to hear it," he said.

"Or maybe you think I don't know my own mind yet? That I'm still just too much of a mess for you to be involved with me?"

That made him sound like a real jerk.

He was trying not to be a jerk here, and yes, not to get involved with anything really messy with a woman who'd just had her life turned upside down.

"You just need some time," he began.

"You didn't think so on the desk in the study at Eleanor's. Or in your office. You could barely keep your hands off me in your office today. And in my room. In my room right next to the kitchen with Eleanor and Kathleen and Gladdy there. Remember that?"

They'd made it to the end of the driveway then, and on the road right in front of them, there went the jogger. He was pretty sure it was the blond-haired trophy wife, staring outright as she moved down the road.

*Great.*

And he still hadn't gotten Lilah in the car. "I'm sorry," he said sincerely. "I'm not saying I don't want you, believe me—"

"But you're not going to let yourself have me?"

"No, I'm not."

It sounded really harsh, and he hated that, but it was his

bottom line. He wasn't going to do this. He knew better. What else could he say?

*Come see me in a year or so?*

She'd slap his face.

"I'm really sorry," he said. "I haven't handled this well."

"No, you haven't," she agreed, but she'd finally stopped walking.

"Please get in the car and let me drive you back to Eleanor's," he said one last time.

She glared at him. Finally, she said, "If you promise not to say another word to me on the drive back…?"

"Deal." He leaned over and pushed open the door for her.

Finally, she got in.

Eleanor had watched happily as Lilah left with the judge and was surprised to see them come roaring back in the judge's car not fifteen minutes later.

"That's odd," she said. "They just left."

"And they don't look happy to be back," said Kathleen, as they stood watching out the kitchen window.

Lilah got out of the car, closed the door none too gently, and the judge started to follow her, but she turned around and told him to stop. "You promised not to say another word."

"On the drive," he said. "We're not driving anymore."

"Really! That's your argument? That we're not driving anymore?"

"Well, we're not."

Eleanor and Kathleen couldn't hear the next few sentences as the arguing couple disappeared around the side of the house. The older women left the kitchen to hide in the dining room just as Lilah and the judge walked in.

"What's to say?" Lilah said. "You don't want to have

anything to do with me. Fine! I got the message. You can go now."

"Lilah, I really am sorry."

And with that, the judge left. Lilah watched him go from the same window where Eleanor and Kathleen had watched them arrive.

"Oh, dear," Eleanor said. "Time to find out what happened."

Kathleen nodded. They marched into the kitchen, ready to act surprised.

"Oh," Eleanor said, "I didn't realize you were here, dear. I thought you'd be a while with the judge."

Lilah sniffled, hastily wiped away tears and said, "I didn't think I'd be back so soon, either, but that man is so annoying."

"Most men are, dear," Kathleen agreed. "What did he do?"

"I really can't say."

"Of course, you can," Eleanor insisted.

"Just think of us as your mother, dear," Kathleen said. "Every girl needs her mother now and then, and yours isn't here. So, tell us. What did he do?"

"He...he...he doesn't want to have anything else to do with me!"

Eleanor and Kathleen gasped together, taken aback. Everything had been going so well.

"I just can't believe that," Eleanor said. "He's crazy about you. He nearly ravished you in the study. Those are not the actions of a man who wants nothing else to do with you, my dear."

"That's what I told him," Lilah said.

"Well, good for you," Eleanor said. "What did he say to that?"

"That he hadn't handled things well, that he's sorry,

and that I hadn't been divorced long enough, if I'm even actually divorced at all."

Eleanor didn't like hearing that. "I thought your divorce was final before you moved here?"

"So did I," Lilah said. "But Ashe seems to think there's some kind of waiting period. A month, maybe two, and that the divorce isn't actually completely final until the end of the waiting period. Although, it could be final now and the papers on the way to me, just not here yet. Still, not even that would be enough to satisfy him."

"Why ever not?" Kathleen said.

"Apparently recently divorced women are too emotional for him, too much of a mess." Her bottom lip started to tremble, her composure hanging by a thread. Finally, she dipped her head down low and buried her face in her hands. "I just liked him so much!"

At which point, both women rushed to embrace her.

"Don't you worry about a thing, dear," Eleanor said. "We'll fix this."

"I don't think so," Lilah said. "He has a very strict policy."

"We'll see about that," Eleanor said.

She and her friends did not give up easily. The judge was no match for the three of them.

## Chapter Eight

The next day, Ashe was in his office when his assistant came in and said there was a messenger outside with instructions to hand deliver a letter to him. That was odd. His assistant would normally take care of such things.

"He says it's personal," she said.

It still seemed odd, but Ashe's life had been so crazy for the past few weeks, he let it go. "Fine. Send the man in."

He signed the young man's clipboard, indicating that he had indeed received the message in person, then took the letter and waited until both his assistant and the messenger left to open it.

Inside, he found a copy of Lilah's divorce decree, dated five days before. Nothing more, just a copy of the divorce decree.

So, she was actually divorced, and she had been divorced when they'd had their latest argument. Still, she'd only been divorced for four days. Four days was nothing.

No time at all. He'd done the right thing in refusing to see her anymore. He knew he had.

It still felt lousy. He decided to send her some flowers, an extravagant arrangement, along with another apology. He didn't know what else to do.

The next day, he was summoned to the estate by Eleanor. No explanation, just a handwritten note, again sent by messenger, making him wonder if Eleanor had been the one to send the divorce decree the day before. So, he'd made Eleanor mad, too, by refusing to see Lilah?

He went after work that evening, because Eleanor Barrington Holmes was not a woman he wanted to have mad at him if he could help it. She brought him through the house and to the back patio, inviting him to tea once again. He was dismayed to find he had to face the entire trio of women. Kathleen and even Gladdy the outrageous were at the table, waiting.

He sat, accepted tea from Eleanor and a few tiny tea cakes offered by Kathleen, then braced himself as best he could. With these three, it was no telling what was in store.

"So, Judge," Eleanor said. "I've decided to throw a little cocktail party for you."

That was a surprise. He just stared at her.

"I'm sure you know I've been quite successful as a fundraiser for a number of candidates over the years," Eleanor said. "I do so love a good party, and I've decided that you're someone I want to help get reelected. You're going to need a lot of money, and I suspect you're one of those people who hates the idea of having to ask people for that kind of support."

"Well, I don't know what to say," Ashe began. "That's very generous of you, Eleanor."

"Not at all," she said. "I plan on enjoying myself very

much, and my friends Kathleen and Gladdy have agreed to help me. That's what people do for friends. They help each other."

That's when Ashe started to feel the slightest bit uneasy. Friends helping friends? Exactly what kind of help was Eleanor referring to?

"Naturally, I'd be happy for any help you offer," Ashe said, then waited to hear what she wanted in return.

"Lovely," Eleanor said. "A week from Thursday would be good for me. Is that good for you?"

Ashe got out his phone, which also held his schedule. The date was clear. Why was he so uneasy about this? Still, he said Thursday would be fine.

"Well, then, that's settled," Kathleen said. "I can hardly wait to start planning. Gladdy and I have a number of friends we want to invite, too."

"Thank you," Ashe said. "I appreciate it very much."

He drank his tea, nibbled on a bite-size crumb cake. There was bound to be something else to this.

"We were so sorry to hear that you and Lilah wouldn't be seeing each other anymore," Gladdy said.

And there it was. They planned to grill him on what had happened between him and Lilah? Had they not been able to get enough information out of Lilah herself?

"But the flowers you sent were just lovely," Eleanor said.

"Oh, yes. I do so love orchids," Kathleen said.

Again, Ashe just sat there. He wasn't going to explain his own dating rules to these three. They stared back at him, clearly wanting something more from him. He tried not to fidget in his seat. He was a judge. They weren't going to stare him down.

"But you are attracted to her, aren't you, Judge?" Gladdy asked.

Okay, the direct approach. Why would that surprise him, when it came to the three of them? "Ladies, I really don't think—"

"I know, it's bad of us to want to be involved in this thing between the two of you—"

"There's really nothing between the two of us anymore," Ashe said.

"But there most certainly could be," Eleanor said.

"I really think this is a conversation to be had between Lilah and me," he tried.

"Yes, we know. It's just so hard, to see poor Lilah so sad. And the two of you seem so happy together," Kathleen said.

"She's a lovely woman," he admitted.

"Yes, she is. And we had such hopes for the two of you," Kathleen said.

"I thought you did. You ladies have been matchmaking, haven't you?"

They smiled. One of them blushed. All of them seemed delighted with themselves. There it was, they'd been trying to set him up with Lilah.

"Ladies, I'm sorry if I gave you the wrong impression. But I've been single for a long time now. I have every intention of remaining unmarried."

Gladdy giggled. "Oh, dear. We weren't trying to get you to marry her."

"You weren't?" Ashe wasn't sure he believed that.

"No, no, no. Not that. Lilah isn't ready for that. She just got out of a bad marriage. The last thing she needs is another one," Eleanor claimed.

And once again, the ladies had surprised him. If they weren't matchmaking, then what were they up to?

"We had other ideas," Kathleen said.

Ashe truly couldn't imagine what those were.

"You see, dear, it's so difficult for a woman, coming out of a bad marriage, particularly a long marriage. She feels like a failure. She feels unattractive, sad, doubting herself and everything to do with men and relationships."

"Exactly," Ashe said. They were in complete agreement. "It's a bad time for any woman to get involved in a new relationship."

"Well, there are relationships and then there are relationships," Eleanor said.

And what exactly did that mean, Ashe wondered?

"I think it's truly important that a woman gets back into the dating scene with the right person, someone who is kind and understanding, patient and attentive. Someone who helps her remember how wonderful it is to be a woman. Someone who finds her desirable and beautiful."

Oh, he hated that thought. He gritted his teeth and said, "I'm sure she'll find a wonderful man—"

"But she has," Eleanor said. "She's found you. And the two of you obviously find each other attractive. She is free of any attachments now, and so are you."

"I thought the three of you weren't matchmaking," Ashe said.

"No, dear. We're not. As we said, Lilah isn't ready for any sort of long-term relationship, and you said you're not interested in anything permanent, either. Which makes you perfect for each other."

"I'm afraid I don't understand," Ashe said. It seemed as if they were talking in circles.

"We don't want you to date Lilah," Gladdy said. "Or begin any sort of long-term relationship."

Okay, good. Ashe was off the hook.

"We just want you to…initiate her back into the ways of single womanhood."

Surely Ashe was mistaken. Surely they weren't asking him to...

"I suspect you're very good in that department," Gladdy said, grinning wildly. "And we want this to be a very good experience for her."

"The last thing she needs is some selfish lout of a man. Another selfish lout of a man, I should say," Eleanor said.

"You're just the man for the job," Kathleen said.

Ashe looked into the three smiling, earnest faces. Three little old ladies were asking him to seduce Lilah? To be her first lover after her divorce? To show her a good time in bed?

It was the most outrageous proposal he'd ever received, so much worse than them trying to play matchmaker. Wyatt had warned him that the three of them were outrageous women, always up to something. But he was sure this was something even Wyatt hadn't expected.

What in the world could he say to them?

And it wasn't helping that the idea was so appealing to him. No commitments, just him and Lilah in his bed, on his desk, against a wall somewhere. He could make sure she remembered what it felt like to be a highly desirable woman, cherished, pampered, indulged.

"You know you want to," Gladdy said.

Ashe choked on his tea, coughing into a hastily applied cloth napkin and still getting a bit of it on his favorite tie.

"Oh, dear. We've surprised him," Eleanor said.

Kathleen dabbed at his tie with her own pristine, white linen napkin.

"We truly have nothing but Lilah's best interests at heart," Eleanor said.

Ashe clamped his mouth shut at first, trying to figure out what to say. "Ladies, I really don't think this is...a proper subject for the four of us to discuss."

"Why ever not?" Eleanor said. "We just adore Lilah, and we think you do, too, Judge. She's in a very vulnerable time in her life, and we just want what's best for her."

"So many women end up jaded, even devastated after a divorce," Kathleen said. "They think they never want another man again, which is such a shame. Men can be difficult, but they have their uses."

Thankfully, she didn't go into detail about their uses to Ashe.

"It's really the perfect solution," Eleanor said. "You and Lilah already know each other. You're clearly attracted to one another. How hard would it be...?"

*How hard indeed,* Ashe thought.

He had to get out of here. Get out now, before they said anything else. Before he said anything else. Before he agreed to anything.

"Just think about it," Kathleen asked.

As if he'd thought about anything but getting Lilah into bed ever since he'd met her. Thinking about it was not the solution.

"It would make me so happy if you did this for us," said Eleanor.

Once again, Ashe could do nothing but stare at her.

"We are friends, aren't we, Judge?" she added. "And naturally, we want our friends to be happy, don't we? And we'll do anything we can to help one another?"

Oh, good Lord. Was the woman bribing him? Offering him her help as a fundraiser in exchange for him seducing her cousin?

Ashe had never been offered a bribe before.

He feared no one in judicial history had ever been offered a bribe like this one, and he really didn't want to make history here. He wanted to forget about Lilah and never have to see these three ladies again. They were too outrageous for words.

The ladies waited and watched until Ashe disappeared around the corner of the house and then erupted in soft laughter, delighted with themselves.

"Oh, my dears, that was perfect. Absolutely perfect," Eleanor said.

"And a brilliant plan, if I do say so myself," Kathleen said.

"Truly inspired. Poor boy, he won't be able to think of anything else, except doing what we asked of him," Gladdy said.

"And once he does that, he won't ever want to let Lilah get away. And then we'll have our match."

Ashe planned on getting out of there as fast as possible, but in front of the five-car garage, he found Lilah admiring a punching bag on a stand. As he watched, she slipped on bright red boxing gloves and started hitting the bag. She winced at the first blow but kept hitting it, eventually seeming to enjoy it. Then she started kicking it.

Ashe wasn't that sure how smart it would be to interrupt her at the moment, but she was standing between him and his car. He couldn't get out of here without her seeing him. So he walked up to her and stood, waiting for her to notice him.

She finally did, glaring at him as she kept hitting the bag. "What are you doing here?"

"I was summoned by Eleanor," he said, getting a funny feeling she was picturing the punching bag as him.

"What for?"

"I think I was just offered a very subtle bribe."

That got her attention. She stopped hitting the bag. "By Eleanor?"

He nodded.

She made a face. "I'm afraid to even ask, but what does she want you to do? And does it have to do with me?"

"It most certainly does." He shoved his hands into his pockets and watched her, watching him. He'd missed her, dammit. Missed her more than he would've liked.

"Well, I can't say I'm surprised. I felt like they were up to something all along, her and Kathleen and Gladdy. For some reason, they seem to like the idea of you and me together. Don't worry, I'll tell them to stop. I don't need anyone playing matchmaker for me."

"That's not exactly what they're doing," he told her.

"Of course it's what they're doing. They seem to think I need help finding a man."

"Yes, finding a man. But I bet it's not for what you think." He was starting to enjoy this just a little bit right now. He'd never seen Lilah shocked, never seen her close to being shocked. Surely this would get her.

"You're a man. What else does one do with a man?" she asked.

"Apparently we have other uses."

She shot him an annoyed look. "Well, I can't imagine what those uses might be."

"They seem to think you need someone to…carefully help ease you back into…let's call it the dating scene."

She pulled off her boxing gloves, let them drop to the ground, crossed her arms and glared at him. "Like…a practice date? I mean, it's been a while, but I seriously doubt I need to practice before I can be trusted to go on a date."

"That's not exactly what they meant."

"Well, just go ahead and say it. I mean, how bad can it be?"

Clearly, she had no idea. He looked her in the eyes. "They want me to take you to bed, to be your first, post divorce."

Her mouth fell open, looking suitably shocked enough to make him happy, at least momentarily.

Then she shot back with, "You're lying."

"I wish I was. Besides, I don't lie, Lilah. If you knew me better, you'd know that."

"Eleanor offered to pay you to take me to bed with you?" she asked, her cheeks flushed prettily.

"More or less."

"More or less? What does that mean, exactly?"

"She offered to host a fundraiser for me, and then talked about what good friends we are, and how friends help friends, and want their friends to be happy. Then she told me she was concerned about you, that women in your position are vulnerable, and that she wanted the first man you're involved with after your divorce to be…how did she put it? Kind, considerate, patient—"

"Oh, my God!" Her eyes got huge, and she looked truly horrified. At least she hadn't known what Eleanor and her friends were up to. "I knew they were a little eccentric. I thought it was kind of fun, how unusual they were and how much they enjoy life. I mean, I hope I'm as happy as they are at their age."

Ashe nodded. As much trouble as they were, they were three very happy ladies.

"I had no idea," Lilah said. "You have to believe me. I didn't know."

"Oh, I believe you. Even you couldn't come up with a scheme as outrageous as this one."

"Well, I'll just tell them to stop. I'll tell them they have to stop. I mean, it's not like they can make us do anything."

"Try that," Ashe said. "And tell me if you get anywhere with them. I tried, but I'm not sure I did."

And then all he had to do was get out of there, not say anything else, not do anything else, such as letting himself touch her. Particularly now that she'd gone back to hitting her punching bag.

"What's with the boxing equipment?" he asked.

"I felt like hitting something. It's a great way to get out your anger without really hurting anyone."

"You wanted to hit me, you mean?" he said.

"Yes, I did."

"And your ex? You still think about hitting him?" Ashe said.

"Not so much anymore. I really did spend the last year wisely, Ashe. I learned a ton about myself, about expressing and then letting go of anger, about forgiveness, about what I want for my own life. But I know it's important to you, so I can promise you, he really is my ex now. I got the divorce decree in the mail the day after I saw you."

"I know. Someone messengered a copy of it to me. Eleanor, I suppose."

Lilah closed her eyes and groaned in frustration. "That woman is amazing."

"Yes, she is. I hope she listens to you more than she listened to me." And then Ashe couldn't think of anything else to say, any other reasons to still be there talking to her, when a smart man would've already left. "Well, I should be going. Good luck with Eleanor."

"Thank you."

## Chapter Nine

Lilah pouted for a few days, pounded her punching bag even more and cursed her ex-husband and Ashe and every man she'd ever wanted but been unable to have. She also watched Eleanor and her friends like a hawk, trying to figure out if they really were sorry about what they'd done or gone back to their old, meddling ways. She'd confronted them after Ashe left, and they'd sworn they'd stop trying to get him to help ease her back into post-divorce sex, but Lilah was still worried.

By the time she had lunch in town with the owner of the lingerie shop, she was ready for some advice, some womanly advice that didn't come from someone who was eighty-something and had asked Ashe to please have pity sex with her.

Just for spite, she asked Sybil, the shop owner, to meet her at the little lunch spot around the corner from the courthouse where she'd had lunch with Ashe. And if he happened to be there, so be it. She could at least try to look good, maybe even sexy, maybe even very sexy and desirable, and make him regret all his silly rules.

Sybil looked like a French seductress, clad in a simple black dress that clung to all her curves, accented with one of those perfectly placed French scarves that Parisian women wore like works of art in the kind of casual knot Lilah could never manage. Heads turned when they walked in.

"We seem to be drawing quite a bit of attention," Lilah said, wondering if people were looking at her or Sybil or both of them.

"The room is full of some of my best customers," Sybil whispered. "Don't let the somber suits fool you."

"You don't mean that some of the men are wearing women's under things beneath their suits, do you?" Lilah said.

Sybil gave a full-throated, sexy laugh. "Well, not too many of them, I suspect. I mean, statistically, it's likely that at least a few of them are, but I can't be sure about anyone in particular. I was talking about them purchasing lingerie for their wives and girlfriends."

"Oh, thank goodness," Lilah said.

"I'm so glad you called me," Sybil said. "Our businesses naturally complement one another. We both help women get on with their lives after being dumped by a man, or dumping a man themselves."

"I mentioned your idea about a field trip to your store to the ladies in my classes, and they're very excited. A little apprehensive, but excited."

Sybil smiled. "I was thinking we'd pick a time when the shop is normally closed, and open up just for you and your clients. I'll have some champagne on ice, some chocolates, show the ladies some of our newest and most popular items, and then they can try things on and help each other pick out some beautiful things."

"That sounds like a fun evening," Lilah said. "We can all use a fun evening."

"Speaking of which, how did your gentleman like the item I helped you pick out?" Sybil said.

"He didn't. Okay, well…he did. He liked it very much. Come to think of it, he still has it—"

"That sounds promising," Sybil said.

"No, not because he took it off me. He stuffed it into his pocket, and then we went to his house. He was going to put it on me when we got there, so he could take it back off. But then he found out my divorce had only been final for a few days, and he freaked out." Lilah gave a disgusted sigh. "He has rules about who he will or won't be involved with."

"Well, don't look now, but he just walked in. And he hasn't taken his eyes off of you."

Lilah smiled but kept looking at Sybil. She'd been hoping all along that he would show up. She'd taken extra care with her appearance. Easing her shoulders back, she took a breath and tried to appear as nonchalant as possible, although she could already feel him watching her.

"You still want him," Sybil said, telling Lilah, not asking.

Lilah thought about it for a moment. Did she want him? "Either I still do or I want to make him sorry for refusing to have anything to do with me."

"Well, either motive works. And for either one, you need to look your absolute best. When are you going to see him again?"

"My cousin Eleanor is giving a cocktail party fundraiser for him on Thursday, but I wasn't sure if I was going or not." She was still uneasy that Eleanor was doing it, although Eleanor claimed she truly believed Ashe was needed on the bench and that it was her civic duty to help keep him there. Granted, her interest in politics had been long-standing and well-known in the community.

"Oh, you're definitely going. And I'm going to help you," Sybil said confidently. "You're going to be dazzling. I think our aim should be to leave him unable to speak, just from the sight of you."

Lilah liked the sound of that. She liked it a lot. Then she remembered… "There's just one little thing." She told Sybil what the ladies had done.

Even Sybil was a bit shocked and surprised, but she took it all in stride. "It is unfortunate, but you shouldn't let anything they've done keep you from getting what you want. So, despite the embarrassment, do you still want him?"

"I'm not sure," Lilah said.

"Well, I don't think you have to decide immediately. I say we proceed as if you do and make sure you look dazzling just in case." Sybil gave a satisfied sigh. "He's a very attractive man, rumored to be excellent in bed—"

"Wait? You know that? You've—"

"Oh, no. Not me. But he's been in my shop before, and women he's been involved with have been in my shop, too, and they confide in me. Trust me, I know all the men in town who are…shall we say…worthy of a woman's attentions. He's definitely one of them."

Lilah decided right then and there that Sybil and Eleanor should never be in the same room together, because it was no telling what sort of schemes they might cook up between them.

Forty minutes later, Lilah was leaving the café, when she felt a hand at her elbow, steering her quickly down the street and around the corner. She thought she knew that hand, or maybe she knew the scent of the man, the way he moved, or some intangible thing about him that made her recognize him instantly.

It was Ashe.

"What are you doing?" she asked.

"What are you doing?" He pulled her into an alcove on a side street where they were nearly invisible.

"I was walking down the street. I'm not allowed to walk down the street now?"

"What were you doing at that restaurant? With that woman?"

"That woman runs a business two blocks away, one I'm told you and many of your friends in the courthouse frequent."

He looked taken aback by that. "One that I frequent? I wouldn't say I frequent the business. I've been inside. I've bought a gift or two."

"Oh, I'm sure you have." Lilah was steaming just imagining all the gifts he'd purchased and all the women he'd given them to.

He glared at her. "Lilah, I said I was sorry. I meant it."

"And while we're on the subject of lingerie, you still have mine. And I want it back. I plan to wear it, for a man who appreciates it and me." Take that, she thought, satisfied to see that he was even more furious now.

He couldn't even speak at first; he sputtered a bit and finally said, "I didn't realize I still had that… What did you call it? A slip? That is not a slip. That is so much more than a slip."

*And you will never see me in it,* Lilah wanted to tell him, childish as that was. *Or take it off me.*

Instead she said, "You're mad because I had lunch with a businesswoman at a restaurant in this town?"

"With her. With the lingerie lady. With half the courthouse staff looking on. In the restaurant where you knew I'd be. I think you're playing some kind of game, and I don't like it."

"I had lunch. A business lunch. Sybil and I are talking about doing business together."

That seemed to worry him very much. "You're going into business with the lingerie lady? What kind of business could you possibly have with the lingerie lady?"

Lilah folded her arms in front of her and glared right back at him. "I don't see how that could possibly be any of *your* business."

He just looked at her, a muscle jumping now and then in his tightly held jaw. "Please don't do anything crazy."

She laughed. "You mean something inappropriate? Something you would think is inappropriate? It's funny how it's fine for you to buy lingerie for any number of women from Sybil, but you're terrified of the idea of me doing business with her? Sounds like a double standard to me."

"Lilah, please—"

"Please what? You said you don't want anything to do with me, which makes this none of your business."

Now she had him fuming even more. Lilah found it wonderfully satisfying to make him so mad. It took a bit of the sting out of Eleanor asking him to have pity sex with her.

"So, if there's nothing more you have to say to me, I'll be on my way." She smiled as sweetly as she could manage and then walked back toward the main drag.

Ashe knew he was in trouble, big trouble. He'd made an unpredictable woman mad. It was one thing to make a normal woman mad but quite another to make a some-times inappropriate, often erratic woman mad.

He went to see Wyatt. He hadn't told his friend about what Eleanor and her friends had proposed to him, but now he didn't see how he could avoid it. So he laid out the whole story to an astonished Wyatt in Wyatt's office.

Ashe ended with, "You have to help me."

Wyatt made a face. "I'm not sure I can. I'm not sure anyone can help you. Eleanor, Kathleen and Gladdy asked you to… What was the phrase? Initiate Lilah into the ways of single womanhood?"

"Do you think I could make something like that up?"

"No. I don't think you could. I don't know that anyone could. I can't believe they asked you that." Wyatt looked truly worried.

"Oh, it gets better."

"Better? I don't see how it could possibly get better. Or worse. You mean worse, right?"

"Yes, worse. They're trying to bribe me into doing it."

Wyatt practically whimpered like a scared kid. "Those three tried to bribe you? Into providing…sexual favors for Lilah?"

Ashe nodded.

"How much did they offer you?"

"A fundraiser for my campaign. Eleanor's throwing me a cocktail party on Thursday, in exchange for me… taking care of Lilah."

Wyatt looked as freaked out as Ashe had ever seen him. "I have to talk to Jane. If anyone can handle Kathleen, it's Jane, and if anyone can handle Gladdy, it's Kathleen. I think Jane is our only hope."

"What about Eleanor? Eleanor's the ringleader."

"We have to hope Eleanor got dragged into this by Kathleen and Gladdy. If Jane can reason with Kathleen, then Kathleen can handle the other two."

"Okay. I can't do this on my own. I've been utterly

defeated by three little old ladies. I'm terrified of them," Ashe confessed. "Them, and a pissed-off Lilah. With lingerie. Lilah has lingerie, and now she's running around town with the lingerie lady, saying they're going into business together. They were talking about it at the café today, right there in the open where anyone could overhear. Where everyone from the courthouse saw them."

Ashe got more freaked out as he talked about it. "You got me into this, and now you have to stop it."

"I had no idea how off base they were going to be," Wyatt said. "I swear I didn't."

"Just fix it," Ashe said. "I don't care what you have to do. Fix it. And get them to cancel this fundraiser. I'm terrified of what might happen if they actually have it."

"How could you let her schedule it in the first place, once you knew what she wanted in exchange?"

"Let her? I didn't let her do anything. Are you under the impression that she waits for permission for anything? I never agreed. Next thing I knew, the damned invitations had already gone out."

It was too late. Eleanor was adamant that she would be having a cocktail party Thursday evening, which she fully expected him to attend. So, despite his fears of what might happen there with him in attendance, he was more afraid of what might happen if he wasn't there to try to control things.

He'd have paid good money to make sure Lilah didn't attend, but he wasn't sure how to make that happen short of kidnapping or bribery, and those were not the sorts of behavior a judge engaged in. So, all he could do was hope she wouldn't be there.

He did have Wyatt beside him. Maybe between the two of them they could handle the little old ladies. Unfortunately, Wyatt's wife, Jane, supposedly their best hope, was still out of town on her book tour.

The two men walked into the large room where the party was held and stood there taking in the scene. Everything looked perfectly normal. The crowd mostly consisted of a bunch of lawyers and local politicians, all dressed sedately, drinking, nibbling on hors d'oeuvres, and talking quietly.

Eleanor saw them and pounced, beaming up at Ashe and taking him by the arm. "Judge, I'm so glad we've come to an understanding."

Ashe shot a pleading look at Wyatt.

Wyatt winced and slid his arm through one of Eleanor's, leaning down to whisper something to her that Ashe couldn't hear. She did not look in the least deterred. So much for Wyatt's help.

Ashe allowed Eleanor to lead him around the room, introducing him to everyone, making sure he shook everyone's hand, while she sang his praises. She was certainly holding up her end of the bargain he never agreed to. Still, it was okay so far. Nothing bad had happened, nothing outrageous.

And then he caught a glimpse of a woman in a little, pale yellow suit. Not the kind of suit women in the legal profession wore. The skirt was just a bit too short, showing off a fantastic pair of legs. Her feet were encased in dainty, high-heeled sandals in the same pale yellow color. The jacket cinched to a tiny waist and then flared up to accommodate what looked like a perfect pair of breasts.

It was Lilah. Even though he'd never seen her in anything like this before, he knew it was her by the clenching of his jaw and the way his heart kicked up a bit, even before he saw her face.

She wore her hair up in an elegant knot atop her head

that showed off the curve of her neck. From the side view he had, she looked more respectable and normal than he'd ever seen her. Why would that scare him?

Still, maybe it was going to be okay, he told himself. Maybe she wasn't so mad anymore.

Then she turned to face him, and he saw what she'd done. She wasn't wearing a blouse under the jacket of her suit. A normal woman would wear a blouse, but not Lilah.

She was wearing a slip. The one that wasn't really a slip. That wickedly sexy piece of lace that he'd never gotten to see her wearing, the one she'd planned to wear for him in private and then let him take off her, either before or after he'd had his way with her. He should never have messengered it back to her a few days ago. He should have known better.

And the crazy thing about it was, she looked almost perfectly respectable standing there in her little yellow suit. In fact, he was likely the only one who knew what she was wearing underneath it, because all anyone saw was a tiny bit of lace showing beneath the deep V-neck of her jacket.

But Ashe did know what it was, and it was driving him crazy.

"She's here," he whispered to Wyatt, who'd come to stand beside him.

"That's her? I thought she dressed like a gypsy."

"She does. Every time I've ever seen her, except for this time."

"She looks great," Wyatt said. "What's wrong? Did she say something?"

Lilah took that moment to give him a wickedly sexy smile as she looked right at him, then took a sip of her drink and turned her back to him.

Ashe started to sweat. He looked at her, and he didn't

see her in the little yellow suit. He saw her in nothing but that scrap of lingerie.

"Please make her go away," he begged Wyatt.

"Why? What did she do? I didn't see anything."

"It's not what she did, it's what she's wearing." Ashe turned his back to her, hoping that might help. It didn't.

"What's wrong with what she's wearing? I like that suit. Jane likes to wear little suits like that. They look so sexy on her. Especially if you know what she wears under them." Wyatt didn't seem in the least bit alarmed.

"That's the problem," Ashe said. "I know what she's wearing under it."

Wyatt frowned. "How do you know? You haven't left this room since we arrived, and neither has she."

"I just know," Ashe said. "Please, help me. You got me into this. I can't be here with her when she's wearing that."

"But I don't—"

"In my mind, I've taken it off her a million times," Ashe admitted.

"Oh," Wyatt said. That was clearly something he understood. "Okay, wish me luck. I'm going in. I'll do my best."

Ashe watched as Wyatt crossed the room, only to be waylaid by Eleanor herself. She took him by the arm and led him into a corner of the room and introduced him to someone Ashe didn't know.

*Great.* He was on his own.

Three people tried to talk to him, and he couldn't follow the simplest train of thought, the simplest conversation. He feared that he looked like an idiot, eventually receiving nothing but puzzled, possibly concerned looks. Wyatt was still on the other side of the room, Eleanor hanging on to him for dear life, and Lilah was flirting with an idiot clerk from another judge's office.

He couldn't stand it any longer. He stalked across the room, stepped between her and the other man, took her by the arm and asked the clerk to excuse them. Then he led her out the back door onto the terrace, stopping behind a huge potted plant, a spot where he hoped no one inside could see them. He intended to ask her what in the world she was trying to do, but he feared he already knew. She was trying to make him crazy.

She stared up at him, and in that instant, he wasn't sure he could speak. He was face-to-face with that little scrap of lace now, and it was messing with his mind even more.

"You just had to wear that?" he asked finally. "Knowing I'd be here?"

"It's a suit. I bought a business suit, because Eleanor said everyone would be wearing a suit." She glared at him.

"You know what I'm talking about, Lilah. That," he said, pointing at it. At least, he intended to point at it. What he ended up doing was touching it. Touching that little scrap of lace, deep in the hollow between her breasts.

She took a breath, which had her breasts rising and falling inside the suit. "The neckline was lower than I expected. I didn't want to be showing too much skin, especially here," she claimed.

He wanted to shake her, to take her by the arms and shake her and then maybe undress her with his teeth. And he wasn't a man who manhandled a woman. Still, maybe he could throw her over his shoulder, haul her to his car and just get her out of here. Before he really did something he was going to regret.

He leaned down close enough to whisper in her ear,

You know exactly what you're doing, and so do I. Please op."

"What do you want me to do? Leave town? Leave the untry? Leave the planet?"

"I want you to stop wearing that ridiculous slip where can see it," he said. He could list a slew of other things needed from her, but never seeing that slip again would a good start.

Lilah smiled in a way that made him very, very nervus. The next thing he knew, she was unbuttoning her cket, revealing more and more of that little slip with ery button.

Ashe started to sweat. "What the hell are you doing?"

"You said you wanted me to stop wearing it. I'm taking off." She had all four buttons of the jacket undone by en and slipped it off her shoulders, leaving her standing front of him in that piece of lingerie he'd never seen on r body before.

It had tiny little spaghetti straps that showed off her le shoulders to perfection, plus all the delicate bones of r chest, a few little freckles here and there, and all that nooth, creamy skin. It dipped down in a deep, sweep-g curve at the neckline, softly cupping her breasts and aving nothing to the imagination except the exact color her nipples.

Ashe was ready to beg, and then he remembered he'd ready begged. Begged her very nicely to please stop rmenting him, and this was what she'd done.

She reached behind her back, and he realized she was abuttoning her skirt, and that it would be the next thing come off. Clearly, she wasn't wearing a bra, so if her tent was to do as he asked and remove the slip, he sup-sed she'd end up standing here in front of him in noth-g but her high heels and a pair of panties.

Please, let her be wearing panties.

He was doomed, that was all there was to it. He put hi body between her and the back of the house, hoping to block anything anyone might be able to see through the plant. And then, because he had to, he grabbed her skir at her waist and held it where it was. He really didn't wan to touch her, not when she was taking her clothes off, bu it was either grab her skirt to hold it in place or let he take it off. And he couldn't let her do that.

"Okay, I give up. I'll do anything you want. Just tel me what it is." He didn't even feel bad about admittin it, or about giving her that kind of power over him. Sh already had it, and she knew it. A part of him was happ to finally be giving in.

"You said you wanted me to take this off. I was goin to take it off—"

"Come on, Lilah. You win. I give up, I just told you so What do you want?"

"Well, I thought I wanted you, but then you said yo didn't want me. And then I mostly just wanted this—t prove to myself that I could make you want me."

He swore softly, insisting, "Wanting you was never th problem. You know that."

She stopped trying to get her skirt off and left him t hold it in place, and then pressed her palms against hi chest and looked up at him. "I guess I'm not sure exactl what I want now. I'm still thinking about it. But this i highly satisfying. You look like your head's about to ex plode."

She rose up on her toes and kissed him softly on th cheek, then fastened her skirt, put her jacket back on, bu toned it up and walked away, leaving him standing there watching her go.

\* \* \*

"You did what?" Sybil asked gleefully later that night as she and Lilah sipped champagne and nibbled on chocolate left over from the cocktail party.

"I took my clothes off. Right here on the terrace behind that giant potted plant," Lilah said, still proud of herself for that. "Ashe said he didn't want me wearing that slip I bought at your store, so I pretended I was going to take it off, right here."

They both giggled outrageously, a product of their delight at Lilah's bravery and perhaps a bit too much champagne.

"What did he do then?" Sybil asked.

"I thought he was going to have a heart attack, right here, and he grabbed my skirt and wouldn't let me take it off."

"Serves the man right. He's probably been getting his way with women for far too long. It's about time someone stood up to him. I'm glad you did."

"Me, too. I felt wicked and powerful. All women should feel that kind of power." Lilah bit into another sinfully delicious chocolate truffle. "But as satisfying as that moment was, I still don't know what I want next with him. I even admitted that to him."

"Nothing wrong with that. He can wait. He's probably not accustomed to that, either."

"True," Lilah agreed.

"You want him, you're just not sure you should let yourself have him, although I don't know why. Think of him as a nice present to yourself. You've been through a difficult time, your ex-husband was a jerk and now you deserve a little treat. Although, I bet he's not a little treat...."

They giggled like schoolgirls.

"You can go back to figuring out what you want for the rest of your life later," Sybil advised.

That certainly sounded reasonable to Lilah, although she admitted, "I'm not sure I have the nerve."

"Darling, someone has to be your first, after the divorce, and you know who you want that to be."

*Oh,* she did. It had been so satisfying to see Ashe off balance earlier. She could enjoy seeing him that way again. Maybe Sybil was right. Maybe she should just consider Ashe a little present to herself and do whatever it took to have him.

## *Chapter Ten*

The following week, Lilah took her class to the lingerie shop. They drank three bottles of champagne, ate three dozen chocolate truffles from Amy's bakery and tried on practically everything in the store, eventually overcoming their modesty and modeling their new finds for the class. Lilah herself even joined in the fun.

Feeling beautiful was the only way to truly be beautiful, Sybil said. The class had taken a vow to do their best to feel beautiful from now on.

Their outing ended with a late supper two blocks away, where with a good deal of laughter and a few tears, the women settled into a discussion about their love lives since their various breakups. For most, it wasn't encouraging. Many had already slept with their exes. The rest wondered if they'd ever so much as go on a date again, much less have sex. But they found strength in each other and all they were learning in Lilah's class.

Lilah was walking to her car when she heard footsteps behind her. It spooked her for a minute, because one of the women in her class was being harassed by an abusive ex-husband, and Lilah thought for a moment he might have followed Erica there or been following her home. Erica had left right before Lilah and was parked just down the street. Lilah had watched to make sure Erica made it to her car, just to be safe. Then she heard the footsteps behind her.

She looked around the street carefully, finding it mostly empty, then stopped directly under a streetlight and turned around, bracing herself for what she might find.

And there was Ashe again.

*Whew.* She blew out a breath, relief flooding through her.

He looked at her sharply, then around at the mostly empty street. "Did I scare you?"

"No," she claimed.

But he didn't buy it. "The woman you needed the cop's name for a while back? Is her ex-husband causing trouble for you?"

"No," Lilah insisted. The man hadn't done a thing to Lilah, although he wasn't happy and Erica was scared she'd spotted him following her a few times.

"Dammit, Lilah. I told you, it's not safe for you to be involved in anything like this."

"It's not safe for anyone. I know that. But she's come to me for help, and I'm not going to turn my back on her now."

"Of course not," he said, as if that was a really stupid thing to do.

"I've been in situations like this before with women who've been abused."

"That doesn't make me feel any better," he said, sighing. Then his attention caught on the bag she carried. "And you've done some more shopping?"

"Class outing," she said.

"You took your whole class to that shop?"

"I did. It was a big hit with everyone. We spent a fortune, but we had a great time and we all have beautiful new things to wear." Let him wonder whom she'd be wearing hers for. "How are you? Heading home?"

He nodded. Small town. Sybil's shop was only a couple of blocks from the courthouse, after all. She was bound to run into him sooner or later.

And then they both just stood there, awkwardness personified.

"Eleanor said your fundraiser went well," Lilah said, finally coming up with something she could say.

"It did. She's really good at getting people to show up and pull out their checkbooks. In fact, if I could just turn my entire reelection campaign over to her, I would."

She nodded, then admitted, "I feel…a little bit bad about…you know…almost taking my clothes off there."

"You do?"

"A little bit. I really don't want to cause trouble for you, Ashe, and I know your job is important to you—"

"It is—"

"You just…sometimes, you seem so disapproving of me and anything I do, and I want to push back at that, at you, to shake you up a little bit—"

"Well, you certainly do that," he admitted.

"And as much as I enjoyed it at that moment…in thinking back on it now, I'll admit, it was a bit…excessive to just start pulling off my clothes that way, in front of all those people you were trying to get to give you money."

He just stood there looking down at her through the darkness. She couldn't tell at all what he was thinking.

"So…" Lilah rushed on, nervous now. "Eleanor said you've shown a decided lack of initiative in your campaign."

"I don't want to campaign. I don't want to fundraise. I just want to be able to do my job and…" He looked exasperated, then finally admitted, "Not miss you. I want to not miss you, Lilah."

"You don't have to miss me. You know exactly where I am." Lilah was pleased with her boldness. She had several glasses of champagne in her and new lingerie.

He rocked back on his heels and frowned. "You think I'm an idiot, don't you? Okay, sometimes I think I'm an idiot, too."

"I think you're a very stubborn man. You've decided I'm too much of a mess for anything between us to be simple, and you're wrong. I doubt anyone ever tells you that, and I also doubt you're so wrong very often. But you'll have to figure that out for yourself. I'm certainly not going to beg you to take me to bed with you."

Now, he looked positively grim. "What are you going to do?"

Lilah stood up a bit straighter and said, "I'm going to get on with my life, and try not to make some of the same mistakes the women in my classes have."

"And what mistakes would those be?"

"The most common seems to be sleeping with your ex-husband. Definitely don't want to do that," Lilah said. "Except when I think about how much it would upset the woman he was cheating on me with. But even the thought of upsetting her isn't enough to make me willing to sleep with him again."

"Good," Ashe said.

"Although apparently a lot of women get lonely enough to do just that. I really can't imagine being that lonely."

"I can't imagine that you would be. You're a beautiful woman, Lilah."

"Thank you, but apparently the dating situation is grim. Men pick up women a dozen years younger and go right on, and women find men a dozen years older are after them." She shook her head. "The world is so unfair."

"Well, I hear it's the in thing now for women to find a younger man," Ashe suggested.

"Trendy, but I doubt all that common. You know, I never even asked, how old are you?"

"Thirty-eight."

She thought he looked absolutely perfect for thirty-eight. No, he looked absolutely perfect for a man of any age. "You're not going to ask me how old I am?"

"I would never ask a woman that question."

"Thirty-one. I won't make you ask."

"So we're not quite the cliché."

Definitely not. He was a man who turned down sex with a woman, after all. Commitment-free sex. Or maybe pity sex.

"So you're heading back out into the dating world?" Ashe said.

She nodded. "Any tips to offer?"

He shrugged easily. "I'd say stay away from newly divorced men, but I'd probably make you mad all over again. Just be careful, Lilah. Don't let yourself be hurt again."

And it hit her like a blow that he was a very nice man, and she missed him. She missed him so much she ached with it at the moment. She missed talking to him, laughing with him, flirting with him and kissing him. And she feared that the next man she found would in no way compare to him.

What in the world was she supposed to do about that?

"I miss you, too," she admitted.

He looked taken aback, his mouth settling into a grim, straight line. And then he looked as if he had no idea what to say. Feeling as if she had nothing to lose, except a bit of her dignity, Lilah leaned forward, rose up on her toes and touched her lips to his.

It was a soft, slow, lingering kiss; at least that's what she meant it to be. She opened her mouth ever so slightly and licked across his soft lips. He groaned, slipped his hands around her back and then down to her hips, and pulled her body firmly against him. His body was big and hard, a sensual heat blasting over her.

He swore as he opened his mouth over hers and plundered inside, like a man intent on feasting on her. A moment later, without breaking the kiss, he backed her up against the brick wall of the building just to their right and leaned into her.

Lilah clung to him, her body starting to tingle all over. She let him do whatever he wanted after that, all the while letting her own hands roam all over him, from that thick, full hair on his head, to the side of his face, to those broad shoulders, down his chest, to his hips, anchoring his body to hers.

His mouth trailed across her cheek down the side of her neck, down between her breasts, and then he nosed his way toward one of her nipples, using his tongue to reach for it beneath her clothes. She arched her body up to his mouth, and he finally got what he wanted, as he pushed her top aside and sucked hard on her breast.

It was heavenly. She had her hands in his hair again, holding his head against her, and with his hands urging her on, she wrapped her legs around his waist. If they weren't careful, he'd be pulling down her panties, unzipping his pants and having her right there in the alley.

Lilah laughed, feeling free and happy and more than a little bit daring. She was breathing hard, as was he, the darkness of the warm night air enveloping them in a little world of their own.

His mouth was still on her breast. She feared he wasn't going to let this go any further, because his mouth had turned patient where it had once been urgent, and the raging desire had given way to a simmering heat. She thought about taking matters into her own hands, about pushing this further, but they were downtown. It was quiet at this time of night but not deserted. If someone saw them and knew who he was...

"We're going to stop," he said, his mouth still on her. "Not right this minute, but we will."

"Whatever you want," she said.

"No, most definitely not whatever I want," he said, sounding mad again as he raised his head and looked down at her through the darkness. "Are you trying to make me crazy? Because if that's your goal, you're doing a really good job."

And then he kissed her again, hard and a little bit angry, and she kissed him right back.

When he finally lifted his head, eased her legs from around his waist and back to where she could stand on the ground, he looked like a man completely undone.

"I don't understand," he said. "Help me understand. Are you like this with everyone?"

"I haven't been with anyone else, not since the divorce, not since the separation, not since I was married, and there really weren't that many men before I was married. So, no, I'm not like this with everyone." She didn't know whether to be furious or puzzled or hurt. "Did I do something wrong? Should I pretend I don't want you, pretend it doesn't feel good to be with you? Should I push you away? Or just make you work a little harder to get what we both know you want?"

He was still breathing hard, pulling away from her in some invisible way. Clearly, he hadn't changed his mind about anything.

"Never mind," Lilah said, shoving him even farther away and taking off down the alley back toward the street and her car.

"Lilah, wait," he called after her.

She kept right on walking. He followed her all the way to her car. She pulled out her keys, and it was only then that he reached out a hand to stop her.

She turned and glared up at him. "Let me guess, nothing's changed."

He shook his head, seeming to be at a complete loss for words. "I'm sorry—"

"I was sure you would be."

And then she got in her car and left.

Ashe made it through three whole days before he went to find Wyatt.

"You think I'm an idiot, don't you?" Ashe said.

Wyatt laughed at him. "We all are sometimes, particularly when it comes to women."

"I can't stop thinking about her," Ashe said.

"Well, you don't have to. I know you have rules about this sort of thing. I'm sure they've served you well in the past. But that doesn't mean you can't ignore your own rules every now and then."

Ashe shook his head. It couldn't possibly be that simple. Forget the rules?

He had rules for a reason. Everyone had rules for a reason. To make things simpler. It helped one avoid complications and mistakes. Ashe didn't like making mistakes. He didn't like complications.

But he wanted Lilah.

Wyatt laughed. "Just think about it."

"I'm not good at ignoring the rules, particularly my own. We're lawyers, for God's sake. Our whole lives are about rules."

Wyatt shrugged. "I'm just saying, no one's going to come arrest you for breaking your own rules. No one's even going to know."

Which meant he could have her. He could have Lilah anytime he wanted, if she wasn't still too mad at him. And even if she was still mad, he could make her forget all about that. He was certain he could.

"Just stop thinking so much," Wyatt said.

"Stop thinking?" he said finally. "All I do is think. I keep thinking about her, and then I think I'm losing my mind."

Wyatt laughed. "Happens to the best of us, I'm afraid. Don't worry. You'll be fine. You'll be better than fine. You may even be happy."

Ashe was still caught up in the idea that it couldn't possibly be that simple. "So what do I do? Just go to her and tell her I changed my mind?"

Wyatt was still laughing. "You'll figure it out. And maybe you'll even get your mind on what you should be doing right now. Like making sure you still have a seat on the bench?"

"I know. I've actually hired someone Eleanor recommended to manage the campaign, although I haven't done much of anything else. Except mostly stay away from Lilah."

"You don't have to live like a monk to get elected," Wyatt argued. "You just can't look like a playboy. I think you can manage that."

"She's just so unpredictable. But I can't ask her to change for me. Her ex-husband did that, and I won't do the same thing to her. And I don't want to put her in a position where someone uses her—makes her look bad or silly or anything less than she is—to take me down. She doesn't deserve that. And that's not the only reason I've stayed away from her. There are a lot of reasons."

He went over the arguments again in his own head. She was vulnerable, confused, didn't really know what she wanted and had a tendency to make him crazy. So why didn't he simply stay away from her? He was an unusually rational and disciplined man. He always did the smart thing.

What was so different about this time?

It seemed the only thing different was her. Ashe had never found a woman irresistible before. He'd wanted women, and he'd had women, all without getting involved in any truly disastrous relationships. After his divorce, he'd been a very smart man where women were concerned. And this was certainly not the time to stop being smart.

But she was very sexy, full of life, bold and kind of silly, smart and kind, and so very sexy. He could tell she was still a little perplexed about her whole marriage and divorce, and he suspected that she was so determined to help other women get through their own divorces as a way of figuring out how to get past her own. Which was smart and kind at the same time, all very Lilah.

He was having trouble keeping his mind on his cases, which was unheard of for him. He was finding no peace in his own home. He was waiting for the day when Eleanor summoned him back to the estate to ask why he wasn't holding up his end of the bargain to bed Lilah. At which time he would have to tell her that she really shouldn't try to bribe judges, that it was against the law, after all.

In short, his life had gone from being reasonable, logical and reassuringly predictable to a mess. And the only thing he wanted to do was something that would surely make it worse in the end.

The only thing he wanted to do was take Lilah to bed.

## *Chapter Eleven*

Ashe was more disgruntled than ever. His orderly, peaceful life was full of her, thinking about her, wanting her, waiting to see what outrageous thing she or her friends did next to throw him completely off balance. She'd even invaded his home, just for those few minutes she'd spent there. He could see her there, remember the taste of her, the smell of her. He told himself that was why he didn't go home but drove instead to Eleanor's one day after work the following week.

Bracing himself as best he could to see Lilah, he got out of the car and headed for the side door. But before he even got there, he heard Lilah's voice in the backyard. Coming around the side of the house, he saw her on the back lawn again with her camera. At least this time, her model had clothes on. He watched her for a few minutes, totally caught up in her work. She had her model laughing, smiling, looking as carefree as a girl.

People were happy around Lilah, he realized. Even he, when he wasn't annoyed or nearly blinded by lust, was happy when she was close. He couldn't take his eyes off the two of them, as he wondered what the new photo shoot was about.

A moment later, Eleanor walked up to him and said, "Judge, to what do we owe the pleasure?"

As if she didn't know.

"I thought I might have a word with Lilah," he said. "But it looks like she's busy. Do you know how long the shoot is supposed to last?"

"It can't last much longer. Lilah has a class tonight, and those ladies should be here soon."

He nodded. It was for the best. He didn't even know what he would have said to her, had she had the time to talk to him.

"Well, I'll talk to her another time," he said. "I don't want to interrupt her shoot, particularly when it seems to be going so well. What kind of class is she planning now?"

"The photo shoot has nothing to do with her classes. She's just doing a favor for...well, I thought it was for you," Eleanor claimed. "You don't recognize the girl?"

"I don't." Ashe frowned. There was something familiar about her, but he just couldn't place her. And he hadn't asked Lilah for any favors.

"Oh, dear. Perhaps it was supposed to be a surprise."

Ashe didn't like surprises, and the whole idea of Lilah surprising him was downright scary.

"It's nothing bad," Eleanor said. "That's the girl who wanted out of the hospital to go home. You heard her case."

"No way." Ashe looked at the girl again. "She was completely bald, pale as could be with big dark circles under her eyes. She looked like she might collapse during the hearing."

But now here she was, laughing and flirting with the camera on the back lawn. She was beautiful. She had a glorious head full of dark blond hair, a beautiful face that was just glowing; she seemed as normal and healthy as could be.

"I don't understand," Ashe said again.

Eleanor frowned. "I think it would be best if Lilah explained. Shall I have her call you after her class tonight?"

"No, thank you. I'll get in touch with her myself."

He went home to work but curiosity and simply the urge to see her took him back to the estate as Lilah's class was ending. One of the women who was leaving told him the class had met on the back lawn around a fire that night.

What in the world was she doing with a fire?

Following the trail of women leaving, he eventually ended up at a campfire tucked away at the very back of the estate. Lilah was the only one left. She sat on a blanket on the ground, her back propped up against a rock, staring into the fire until she saw him. She looked surprised and maybe a little happy.

And beautiful, of course. She always looked beautiful. Her hair was down, long and curly and just a little bit wild, the reflection of the flames catching the reddish tint to it. She had on one of her little spaghetti strap tops and her flowery skirts. With her bare feet and bare arms, she looked so inviting. He was ridiculously happy just to be standing ten feet away from her.

"This is a surprise," she said.

"So is this," he said looking from her to the fire. "Please tell me this is not some ancient, pagan ritual, that you're not dancing naked under the full moon or something."

She laughed, the sound ratcheting up the desire he felt simply at the sight of her. "No one was naked tonight, and the full moon is still a week away. Although I do love the moon, especially when it's full. It looks particularly big and bright back here where there aren't any lights, other than the fire."

He stood there looking down at her. "So if it was a full moon, you'd be here?"

"Ashe, you don't take the time to admire the moon every now and then? Especially when the weather is as perfect as it's been lately?"

"I'm afraid I haven't been giving the moon much attention lately," he admitted.

"Have a seat," she said patting the blanket beside her. "Give it chance. It's a beautiful night. I'm sure you'll like it. You might even find it relaxing. Do you ever do anything just to relax?"

"I'm sure I do." Not that he could think of anything right then. He sat down on the blanket beside her, not too close, leaned back against the rock and looked at the moon, admitting, "It is pretty."

It hung low in the sky, just above the treetops, glowing a soft yellow, about three quarters full, he supposed. The night air was cool but not cold, with the smell of the fire and the sound of it crackling pleasantly. All in all, it was a perfect fall night.

"I dropped by earlier and saw your photo shoot," he said finally. "Eleanor said the girl was Wendy Marx. What are you doing with her?"

"A favor. That's all."

"A favor?" He needed more than that.

"I just couldn't stop thinking about her, after you and I talked about her, especially when you mentioned how much she wanted to look normal."

"Yes. I still don't understand what that has to do with you."

"She doesn't just want to look normal. She's a teenage girl, Ashe. She wants to look pretty. And I know how to do that. I always shoot my own promo material, so I know people who do makeup. Sybil and I took her shopping and helped her pick out an outfit, and a friend of a friend of mine is a costumer on Broadway. She provided the wig. A really good one. Apparently, it's hard to find a wig that looks good unless you have a ton of money to spend. Wendy was thrilled with the wig."

"I didn't even recognize her," he admitted.

"She looked great, didn't she?" Lilah was beaming. "And she was so happy. I think there's a boy she wants to look nice for, but it was for her parents, too. She said she's bald and looks sick in every photo they have from the past three years, and it makes her parents sad to look at them. She wanted them to have a photo that wouldn't make them sad, one where she looked normal and pretty. And maybe she was thinking of what might have been for her if she'd never gotten sick, the girl she would have been."

Lilah was smiling through her tears by the time she was done.

"You went to a lot of trouble to set this up."

"No," she insisted. "It was a phone call or two, a shopping trip and then a couple of hours for the photo shoot. The hardest part was waiting for the wig to arrive. But why wouldn't I do it? For a girl who's been through so much? I was happy to do it, happy to make her smile, even if it was just for a little while."

Of course, why wouldn't she?

She was a nice person, she liked helping people, even if she made him crazy.

"Is this…a problem for you?" she asked finally.

"No." He was embarrassed he'd made anything of it. Obviously it wasn't what he'd thought, some way to manipulate him.

"Are you sure?" she asked. "Because you came here, and I doubt you would have done that if you weren't concerned about something. We've been avoiding each other quite successfully."

"We have been." And he'd missed her. "It's just…Eleanor said something about you doing this as a favor for me."

"Maybe a little bit," she admitted. "I know it was really hard for you to have to handle her case, and you seem frustrated about how little you thought you'd done for her. Which is absolutely wrong, by the way. She couldn't stop talking about you. She said you listened to her, when no one else would, and you got her parents to give her what she wanted, which meant a great deal to her, I promise you. You did a very good thing, Ashe."

He wanted to believe that, but it was hard. He felt as if he'd done so little, that there was so little anyone could do for Wendy.

"I'll admit, I was thinking about you when I offered to do this for her," Lilah said. "I thought it would make you happy that she was happy."

And then, Ashe was at a complete loss for what to say. She wasn't trying to force herself into his life. She was trying to be nice to a sick girl and maybe make Ashe feel better about a really lousy situation.

"Was I wrong to do what I did?" Lilah asked finally.

"No. Of course not."

"Then what's wrong?" she asked.

"Nothing. Nothing's wrong. I'm glad you did it. And it was very nice of you. Thank you."

"You didn't think I was capable of being nice?" Lilah asked. "Ashe, you look so uncomfortable. Clearly, something is wrong. Otherwise you wouldn't be here."

He groaned, shook his head and looked up at the moon, thinking he might find the answers in the sky somewhere. "I was just surprised," he admitted. "I don't... The job isn't an easy one, and it's one where you tend to be alone with the questions, the decisions, your frustrations over what you can and cannot do. This was an especially difficult one. It just felt..."

As if she'd been trying to help him, to take care of him in a way.

And Ashe wasn't a man accustomed to being taken care of. He didn't need anyone to take care of him. He was perfectly capable of taking care of himself, completely self-sufficient and confident in his abilities to handle whatever came his way.

So, it seemed odd to have someone looking out for him, trying to ease the path he walked in some small way. It felt good, too, satisfying deep down. Lilah was definitely trouble and could be silly, but she wasn't particularly demanding or high maintenance. She was surprising, unusual, fun and now, he saw, thoughtful and kind.

He didn't quite know what to do with that.

"Did it really make you that uncomfortable?" she asked. "Because—"

"No, it's fine. More than that, I'm glad you did it, grateful for anything that helps make that girl happy. You did good, Lilah."

She beamed up at him. "Good. We all had a great time with her. She's very sweet, and so smart."

"Yes, she is."

And then, he simply didn't know what to do. He wanted to sit here and admire the moon with Lilah on this beautiful autumn night. Actually, he wanted to do more than that, as he always did when he was close to her.

"No matter what, I can't stop thinking about you," he confessed.

"That's...just awful," she said, grinning broadly.

"It's not easy. Wyatt thinks I'm an idiot."

"I've never liked Wyatt more," Lilah said. "Are we still stuck on your silly rules?"

He nodded.

"You never break them?" she asked.

"No." He laughed. It felt so good to laugh, especially with her. She made him laugh more than anyone, he realized. When he wasn't imagining having her against a brick wall in an alley just off Main Street.

"Have you ever considered, Judge, that perhaps you're simply wrong about this one small thing?" Lilah suggested.

"I'll admit, I've been told one of my greatest failings is that I always think I'm right." At the moment, he wondered what would happen if just this one time, he ignored all those silly rules of his and went with the deep down knowledge that this woman might have the power to change everything about his life, for the better.

But the most insistent thought at the moment was how much he wanted to touch her, kiss her, hold her close and whether he could still walk away without stripping her bare in the moonlight and having her.

*Damn.*

"I have to go," he said.

"Of course, you do," Lilah said. "We wouldn't want anything to happen that you didn't want to happen."

"Would you like me to walk you back to the house?" he asked.

"No, thank you. I'm going to sit here awhile longer. It's too nice a night to waste."

He nodded. "Again, thank you for what you did."

"You're welcome."

And he did it. He walked away without ever touching her.

Lilah was glum the following week.

Her classes were going well, her clients making progress. Eleanor and her friends were as delightful as ever. And Lilah was a completely free woman. She even had the paperwork to prove it. She was enjoying the time she spent with Sybil and thrilled with how beautiful Wendy Marx looked in the finished photographs. Other than the situation with Erica, her student whose ex-husband was becoming increasingly angry and a bit scary as their divorce date got closer, everything was great.

But she missed Ashe. She especially missed teasing him until he grabbed her and kissed her and told her she was making him crazy. But that could only be fun for so long, and then it just got annoying and frustrating. She got so desperate for advice she finally went to Eleanor.

"What do you think I should do?" she asked. "Wait him out?"

Eleanor frowned. "I'm embarrassed to admit I really don't know. I thought this was going to be so easy. For the two of you, I mean. He seemed crazy about you from the start. But he's a silly stubborn man."

"He seems so alone sometimes," Lilah said. "Does it ever seem to you like he's lonely? Like it's not just women that he keeps at a distance?"

Eleanor considered that for a moment. "Well, that doesn't surprise me. He grew up in this town and not under the best circumstances."

That was news to Lilah. "What do you mean?"

"I think it's best that you let him tell you, dear. It's no eat secret, not to anyone who's lived here since he was boy. Let's just say he didn't have the most stable home vironment, that he's definitely a completely self-made an."

"I find myself wanting to do more than just tease him d tempt him. Sometimes, I just want to wrap my arms ound him and hang on to him," she admitted. "Be- use he works so hard and the work he does is so hard. wonder who takes care of him, because it seems like ) one does. I would have thought I'd learned my lesson, om my first marriage, about giving so much of myself take care of a man and make him happy."

"Oh, my dear," Eleanor said. "It's not always a bad ing to take care of a man. I know it sounds terribly old- shioned these days to say such a thing, but it's true. It all epends on the man. Taking care of a good man, a man ho takes good care of you and loves you in return, is ery different than what I suspect you had in your first arriage."

"You're right. My husband wasn't a good man, not to e. And he didn't take care of me. I feel like Ashe would, he'd just let himself into my life."

"And the judge, I believe, is a very good man," Elea- or said. "One worth waiting for, I'd say."

Lilah thought he was; stubborn, opinionated, but good the core. "So, there's nothing I could do to move things ong between us?"

"Let me think about it, dear. I'll ask Kathleen and laddy, too. If anyone can come up with a plan to fix is, it's the three of us."

Which under any other circumstances would have ared Lilah, but she was desperate. She was going to sic three outrageous little old ladies on him, and she didn't even feel guilty about it.

Poor Ashe. He didn't stand a chance.

Ashe drove home beneath a moon that seemed as full and bright and beautiful as could be, and of course thought about Lilah. Was she out on the back lawn of the estate sitting by the fire, staring at the same moon? He supposed she was—she'd told him how much she loved the full moon. And he fought the urge to drive over there and find her that was almost more than he could stand. She would be especially beautiful in the moonlight. All he had to do was turn the car around and go to her. She'd made it clear that she was his for the taking.

He might have done that, except when he pulled into his own driveway, her car was already there, which was odd. She'd never come here on her own. He glanced into the car. Nothing seemed amiss. He looked around the front of the house, all of which seemed perfectly normal. A judge couldn't be too careful about personal security in these times.

With his keys in his hand, he locked the car with the click of the remote, unlocked the front door, but didn't key in the code to disarm the security system right away. First, he scanned the interior of the house, finally spotting Lilah sitting on the brick patio in back. Then he reset the alarm system and walked outside, where she was curled up on the big, comfy, outdoor sofa.

She had on one of those long, flowery skirts of hers and a simple, skimpy top with spaghetti straps that showed off the pretty curves of her shoulders and neck. Her feet were bare, her sandals on the patio beside her. Her hair was long and loose and wild, and she had big tears in her pretty eyes. In fact, it looked as if she'd been crying for a while.

"Did you hear?" She sounded absolutely heartbroken.

He sat down beside her, turning his body toward hers, a hand brushing the hair back from her face. "Hear what? Are you okay? Are you hurt?"

She shook her head, her expression hidden among all that glorious hair again. He felt almost frantic to know what was wrong, to know that she was all right.

"Lilah, you're scaring me. What is it? Did something happen to Eleanor?" Because he knew that would be devastating to her.

"No," she said, her voice breaking on the word. "Eleanor's fine. It's Wendy. She's gone. Sometime yesterday. Eleanor heard about it from a friend who's on the hospital board."

"Wendy?" He closed his eyes, having a hard time thinking that it could be real. "It's barely been a month since she got to go home. She was supposed to have more time, a lot more time. Twice that at least, maybe three times as much."

Tears poured out of Lilah's eyes and down her cheeks. Ashe tried to catch them all and wipe them away, but he couldn't. There were too many.

"They said she must have slipped away in her sleep. No one heard a thing or even realized she was gone until her mother went in to wake her to give her some medicine. She was just gone. It's so sad."

And then Ashe couldn't say anything at all. It was too awful. He lifted Lilah onto his lap and into his arms, held her while she cried her eyes out. It was as if she was crying for both of them, crying all the tears he wouldn't allow himself.

That poor, sweet, sick girl, gone. He felt as if something inside of him was splitting open, all of these feelings spilling out of him, and all he could do was sit there and hold Lilah, who was absolutely heartbroken. He tried to breathe deeply and slowly, calm down, maintain some kind of control. It wasn't working. It seemed hard simply to stay within his own skin, as if all the feelings inside of him couldn't be contained within his body any longer.

Lilah snuggled against him, her face buried against his neck, her cheeks wet against his skin. Although he held her as tightly as he could, it didn't seem to be enough. Nothing did.

Somehow, he decided the most important thing in the world was to make her stop crying. He couldn't handle her sobs any longer. So he tried stroking her hair, running a hand up and down her back, drying her tears himself with his hand. They just fell faster. He couldn't keep up.

He leaned down and pressed his cheek to hers, and then his cheeks were wet, too, with her tears and maybe some of his own. "Lilah, please," he begged. "Please, don't cry anymore."

She took a shuddering breath, sniffled. "I'm sorry. I can't stop."

She was shaking all over, he realized, despite how tightly he held her, and she felt cold to the touch. He couldn't seem to warm her up.

He turned his head ever so slightly, pressed his lips against her cool, trembling mouth, tasting her tears there, too. She sat perfectly still against him, more tears falling down into the crease where their lips met. He caught them with his tongue, licking them gently off her mouth, her cheeks, her beautiful eyes.

"Stop," he begged, feeling insane with the need to halt the pain she was feeling, as if comforting her, taking care of her, was the most essential thing to him.

He kissed her again, really kissed her this time, parting her startled lips and insisting on being allowed inside. He was gentle but determined. She needed to know she wasn't alone. Neither one of them was alone, and he wasn't going to leave her here, feeling so bad.

She didn't do anything at first, simply sat there in his lap leaning heavily against him, letting him do what he wanted. In his head, he could hear his own voice chanting, *Stop, stop. Please, please stop.* He wasn't sure if the words were for him or for her. Not that it mattered, because neither one of them seemed to be listening.

He just kept kissing her, wiping her tears away with his fingertips, running his hands over her body in a way that he hoped was comforting and maybe a little bit distracting. He simply hated the way she was shaking and felt desperate to stop that, too.

He redoubled his efforts at distraction, his hand slipping beneath her top and tunneling up to cup her breasts, small and impossibly soft, perfect, he thought, as he abandoned her mouth, to let his lips slide down the side of her neck, her chest, nuzzling, searching beneath the soft cotton, until he found the curves of her pretty breasts. He teased them with his tongue and pushed with his hands until one of her nipples popped up above the neckline of her top. He captured it with his mouth.

He had her attention then. She arched against him, leaning her head back, giving him easier access, and wrapped her hands around his head, her fingers in his hair, to hold him there, against her.

He took his time, savoring the taste of her, the smoothness, the softness of her skin, the way she smelled, the way it felt to have her hair falling around his face. He felt the cool night air around them, that darkness of night closing in, the peace, the solitude. This was better, so much better.

He put his hands at her waist, lifted her up, eased her thighs apart and repositioned her on his lap, so she was straddling him, instantly aware that he was heavily aroused, and so was she. She fitted her body to his, pressing herself intimately to him, heat to heat, with just a bit of clothing between them.

He peeled off her top in one motion, freeing her breasts completely, attacking them like a starving man. She whimpered, her hands clutching at his head, her hips thrusting against him in a motion that nearly paralyzed him with pleasure. Made him want to do nothing but sit there and feel. He wanted her to feel just as good, so he kept working over her body, his hands finding the edge of her long skirt and pushing it up, above her knees, her thighs, to her waist. His palms cupped her hips, her glorious, soft, warm, bare skin.

He thought for a moment she wasn't wearing any panties, but then realized she was. A thong, nothing but the barest scrap of material, covered her. He could have exploded just thinking about it, but he had to think. He really had to think about this.

Ashe lifted his head and looked around. It was almost dark, and the back of his house sat farther back on the lot than most, a thick stand of trees behind it, all the privacy they needed, he decided. For weeks, he'd been walking around with a condom in his wallet, like some damned schoolboy, just in case he started something between them that he actually let himself finish.

And he was going to finish this.

He rolled her sideways onto her back on the thick sofa cushions, hooked two fingers through the tiny waistband of her panties and got rid of them. Then he knelt between

er legs, unbuckling his belt, unzipping his pants and
shoving them and his boxers down.

He'd meant to grab his wallet and the condom first, but
he got distracted by the sight of her, her hair wild as it
spread out along the cushions, her eyes red and still wet,
lips swollen from his kisses, breasts bare. Her legs were
splayed open, her skirt bunched around her waist, and he
could see reddish-brown curls between her legs. She was
so pretty, so wild and free.

He wanted to do more before he touched those curls,
but didn't think he had the patience, not this time. He
reached out with his hand and stroked her intimately, teasing and making her writhe and arch her body into his
touch. He kept his touch light, even though it nearly killed
him, letting her beg and whisper his name and nudge her
body into his teasing fingers, until he finally gave her
what she wanted, pushing inside with two fingers.

She cried out so loudly, he practically fell on top of her
trying to cover her mouth with his and mute the sound,
and in doing that, he needed both hands to keep himself
from crushing her, and then…

"Ah, dammit," he said. His hard, aroused body was
right there at the warm, wet opening of hers, as if it had a
mind of its own, heat seeking heat. "Lilah, don't move…"

But she did. She rocked her hips against his ever so
slightly, her hands clutching at his shoulders, lips finding his. He rocked just a bit against her, slipping inside
of her just a bit, just the tip of him. He should have told
her right then. *I don't have a condom. I never got it on.*

But she spread her thighs even wider, wrapped her legs
around his waist and raised her hips up to his. He didn't
mean to, really he didn't, but between what she was doing
and what he wanted so badly, he found himself slowly but
surely, deep inside of her.

Ashe groaned and tried to hold back, but she was perfect, her body gripping his, tight but so hot and wet. He suspected it had been a while since she'd done this, and he could have wept at the pleasure of it.

Even that voice inside his head going, *Get out! Get out! Get out!* couldn't sway him. He thrust once, easily but firmly, then again, awash in the most exquisite sensation. She kept moving against him, rocking, arching her body. Clearly, she wanted more.

He finally just let himself go, let him have this, have her. He could do this and still get out in time. It wasn't much, but all he could figure out in the moment. And the moment was just so very good, exquisitely good, nothing but sheer, near-blinding pleasure. He didn't feel anything except her soft, supple skin, pretty curves, eager hands and mouth, tight, wet heat.

He set a deep, steady rhythm that had her bucking beneath him, trying to get him to speed up or slow down or just do something, other than what he was, which was to drive her right over the edge. She cried out, her body shuddering around his in a climax that went on and on and on. He took her mouth with his again, trying to capture the sounds she made.

He felt his own climax come roaring through him. He meant to pull out, to at least do that much to protect her. But her soft hands slipped down to his hips, holding him to her. She arched up against him once more, and he was lost. Utterly and completely lost inside of her.

He buried his face against her neck, trying to muffle the sounds he couldn't hold back. His whole body shuddered, again and again, until he collapsed heavily on top of her, completely spent, barely able to draw breath, his heart threatening to pound its way out of his chest, as he could do nothing but lie there in her sweet, eager arms.

* * *

When she finally opened her eyes, Lilah knew she was outside by the smell of the fresh air and the feel of the breeze on her skin. She was cold on one side and wonderfully warm on the other.

Because of Ashe.

She was here with Ashe, naked and sprawled out on top of him on the outdoor sofa on his patio, dazed and exhausted and very, very happy.

She raised her head just a bit, and his hand instantly cupped her head and urged it back down to his chest. Another of his hands played lazily with her bare hip.

She could have laughed so hard she cried, she was so happy.

*Ashe.*

Then she remembered why he'd done it and sobered up instantly, guilt moving in. Guilt because Wendy was gone, and Lilah dared to feel so happy. Guilt because all Ashe had meant to do was get her to stop crying. She knew that, and wondered if he'd regret this the minute he actually woke up or maybe even be angry that it had happened at all.

But then, he opened his eyes, gave her a dark, lazy, sexy look. He blinked once, then again, then looked around, realizing where they were.

"You must be cold," he said, seeming concerned.

"Not really," she said.

But he didn't seem to believe her. He looked over and found her skirt lying on the patio, picked it up and spread it out on top of her, then sat up with her in his arms, eased her off his lap and onto the sofa.

She clutched the skirt around her, grateful for its length and the abundance of fabric to it, as he found his pants and pulled them on, zipping but not fastening them. Then he reached for her, lifted her into his arms and carried her across the patio, into the house, through the living room, down the hall and into what must be his bedroom.

He didn't bother with the lights. From what she could tell in the dark, the room was neat and tidy, minimally furnished with a leather chair, a chest of drawers, dresser, nightstands and a giant, platform bed with a cushioned, leather headboard with a crisscrossing nail-head pattern.

He started to lower her to the mattress, but she turned her head toward his bathroom. "Give me a minute," she said, and he carried her to the door and lowered her feet to the floor. She gave him a nervous grin, avoided his eyes for all but a second, and then closed the door with him on the other side.

A moment later, she'd rinsed her mouth, splashed water on her face and was staring at herself in the big mirror, her eyes huge, hair just everywhere, the skirt wrapped around her, her only covering.

"What in the world have you done?" she whispered to her own reflection.

Finally, she found the courage to walk out of the bathroom, only to find him waiting anxiously on the other side of the door, a million questions in his eyes.

"Do you want me to leave?" she finally asked him.

"No." His jaw went tight, a muscle jumping in his cheek. "Do you want to leave?"

"No," she said.

He reached for her, taking her by the shoulders, his hands gentle but firm as he waited for her to look at him. "But I would really love to hear that you're on some kind of birth control."

"Oh." She hadn't given it a second thought, not until he'd asked right then. "I am. After we… It seemed like, sooner or later, you and I... I am. You don't have to worry about that. And I had every test there is, after I found out my ex was cheating on me. I'm good."

"Me, too," he said, not looking nearly as relieved as she would have thought.

That surprised her. "You didn't... I mean, we didn't..."

"No. I'm sorry, Lilah. I'm so sorry. There's really no excuse for that."

She just looked at him.

"I was seeing someone who moved away more than six months ago," he said. "And I haven't...there hasn't been anyone since then. I had a complete physical two months ago."

Now, that was even more astonishing.

Six months? For a man like him, that seemed like an eternity, although what did Lilah really know about any of this? She'd been married for ten years to a man she'd met when she was a freshman in college.

"You're perfectly safe, I swear," he tried again.

"Okay," she said.

And then they just stood there, staring at each other, Lilah not knowing what to do next.

Finally, Ashe took her hand and said, "Come to bed with me?"

She nodded, following him to bed, where he drew back the covers for her, let her climb in and then took her skirt from her, slowly uncovering her to his gaze, and tossed her skirt aside. She watched his face as he did it, watched his eyes follow that line of the material as it slid across her body. She could feel his gaze like the touch of a hot, teasing hand, sliding across her skin, following every curve.

He took his time looking at her, and then he slowly undressed himself again and climbed into bed with her, taking her into her arms.

* * *

Ashe thought maybe he was insane, waking up the next morning lying on his side, with his arms and legs wrapped around Lilah, the back of her body spooned against the front of his.

He forced himself to roll away from her and onto his back, close enough to feel the heat of her body but not anything else. She murmured a protest, then rolled half onto her belly and buried her face in the pillow, sleeping on.

*Get up and get out,* he told himself.

Shave, shower, dress, out the door.

He could leave her right here in his bed, leave a pot of coffee brewing and a note, telling her to take her time this morning, to sleep in if she liked, that he was sorry but he just had to get to work, that he was expected in court.

And say nothing about anything else.

Like what they'd done, why he'd done it or how he felt about it. What it meant. He winced at that thought. *What did it mean?*

He couldn't let it mean anything. He hadn't meant to do it, but they had. And, oh, yeah…he wanted to do it again. As soon as possible. Many, many more times, but none of them could mean a damned thing, either.

He feared that wouldn't go over well with Lilah or her three scheming, meddling guardians, even if he'd now done what they claimed they wanted him to do. Initiate her back into the ways of newly single womanhood. Except he'd forgotten to use a condom and hadn't spelled out the whole it-doesn't-mean-a-thing bit beforehand, bungling this colossally, spectacularly, completely.

Ashe, a man who never failed at anything.

He touched a hand to his head, feeling hungover and

sluggish. Did men get hungover from too much really great sex? From stupidity?

He got out of bed and managed to clean up and get ready for work. As he pulled on his shirt, buttoned all the buttons and tied his tie, he stood there by his bed, watching her.

She was a restless sleeper, had been moving this way and that the whole night without ever waking up. Now, she was sprawled out on her belly, a bare foot peeking out from under the covers on one side of the bed, most of her back bare.

He wanted to sit down on the bed and stroke all that bare skin and then uncover some more and stroke that, too.

Ashe frowned, feeling unsettled and all out of sorts. He knew how to do this, and this wasn't the way. He shouldn't still be thinking about her, still be wanting her, not already. He should go to work and do his job, knowing there was a time and a place for everything, and this was the time for work, not sex.

Finally, he made it out of the bedroom, had a cup of coffee, and left the rest of the pot warming for her.

Outside, he gathered up all their clothes from the patio. He tossed his into the clothes hamper and neatly folded hers and left them on the counter in his bathroom, along with fresh towels. On the bed, he left a thick terry cloth robe for her.

Then came the note.

He had to leave a note.

She had to at least have the alarm code, so she could reset it when she left. And he couldn't just say, *Here's the code. Reset it when you leave.*

He found a notepad and a pen, then stared at the blank slip of paper.

*Thank you.*

*I'm sorry.*

*I didn't mean to.*

*Be back by six-thirty. Want to meet me here? We can do this again.*

All of those things popped into his head, all immediately rejected.

*Due in court. Make yourself at home. Please set the alarm when you leave. The code is 63696. Ashe.*

Best he could do, and he really did have to go.

He'd send flowers, he decided. Women liked flowers. Lilah reminded him of wildflowers, a crazy, lush, colorful armload of wildflowers. She'd like those, wouldn't she? But then he'd have to decide what to say on the card, the only flaw to his plan.

He could call her instead, but then he'd still have to decide what to say, and the damned woman didn't understand any of the rules. He was sure of it. He could just stay away from her, not say a thing, but that would make him a cad, and he wasn't that. Just…lost, bewildered, insane.

He settled for the flowers. He'd phone in the order when court broke for lunch, and maybe by then, he'd have figured out what to say.

## Chapter Twelve

Ashe meant to stay at his desk all day, catching up on some work he'd taken home the night before but hadn't done, eating a sandwich in his office and calling the florist about the flowers.

But as he called the lunch break in court, he found himself restless, wondering what she was doing, how she felt about...everything this morning. She hadn't called. He knew because he'd checked his cell phone, his message machine at home and with his secretary. And he still didn't know what he wanted to say to her, not even on a card attached to a bouquet.

So he walked across the street and down the block to the florist he used. He entered and stood there, staring at all it had to offer.

"Judge Ashford," the owner, a woman in her fifties, said as she walked toward him, looking surprised. "You hardly ever actually come into the shop."

He shoved his hands into his pockets and shrugged. "It was a nice day to take a walk."

She nodded. "What can we do for you today?"

He hoped he didn't sound completely ridiculous when he asked, "Do you have any wildflowers? Or...things that look like wildflowers? I don't care what kind, just...colorful and...happy?"

*Exuberant,* he would have said if he wasn't feeling so self-conscious. *Joyous. A little outrageous.*

"She likes bright colors," he settled for saying.

The florist nodded. "Come with me."

He pointed out a number of things he thought were pretty and colorful, that reminded him of Lilah, and the florist promised she could do something very nice with them, then offered him the card to write himself, which took him a ridiculous amount of time. He could feel the looks the people working in the store gave him, as he thought and thought and thought of what to put on the stupid note. As if anyone ever said anything truly monumental on a tiny florist's card. He wondered if they'd open up the card and read it before delivering it.

And then, when he started to pull out his wallet to pay, he remembered Wendy Marx.

"I need something else," he said. "For a young girl. Fifteen. What does a fifteen-year-old want?"

"Roses, would be my first guess. Every girl dreams of a boy who'll give her roses one day. If she's that young, I'd say blush pink, maybe very pale lavender roses," the florist said.

"Fine. For a funeral," he said, wondering if a boy had ever sent Wendy Marx flowers. "I'm not sure where—"

"Wendy Marx?" the florist guessed. "We've sent quite a few arrangements already. But don't worry, we can still get them there in time."

"Thank you. The service is today?"

"Five o'clock, I believe."

*Damn.*

Would Lilah want to go? He certainly didn't.

She could go by herself, come back and cry in his arms and he could carry her off to his bed again. They could help each other try to forget once again that a young girl had died, and that they were not supposed to be together. That thought was cynical as hell, even for him. But it was the first thing he thought of. If Lilah was sad enough, he could have her? What kind of justification was that? The woman cried, and he could do anything he wanted?

But she would want to go to the funeral, and it would definitely make her cry. And then who would she turn to?

"Anything else we can do for you, Judge?" the florist asked.

He realized he'd been standing there staring into space.

"No, thank you. That's it."

He paid for the flowers and left.

Lilah slept decadently late, finally slipping out of Ashe's house, and into and then almost as quickly back out of Eleanor's house, intending to stay as busy as possible running errands in town, all the while trying to keep from thinking about nothing but Ashe.

He'd surprised her.

First, that he'd let himself have her in the first place, because he'd seemed so determined that he wouldn't. Next, because in bed with him she'd expected a certain level of polish and pure skill, but a bit of detachment, too. Not raw hunger and need and emotion, although that had been even sexier and more satisfying than what she'd anticipated. She had a feeling he wouldn't be happy to have let her see any of those particular emotions.

Those big, hot hands of his that could be so gentle and yet at times hard and insistent, taking exactly what he wanted. The look in his dark, weary eyes, the sad expression on his beautiful face. That gloriously fit, hard body and the softness of his hair.

She was astonished and very, very happy. She hadn't ever had any kind of sexual encounter that came close to being as intense and satisfying and thrilling as that night she'd had with him. Although, his ego aside, she doubted he'd want to hear anything like that from her, either.

It all went around and around in her mind, nothing able to stop it until she walked past a downtown flower shop and realized she needed to send flowers to Wendy Marx's funeral.

Inside the shop, a florist was putting together a particularly beautiful arrangement, full of delicate colors and textures, reminding her of a field of wildflowers. She thought she recognized bergamot, Queen Anne's lace, purple coneflowers, goldenrod.

"They're gorgeous," Lilah told the florist, who caught her staring.

"Thank you," the woman said. "I'm Anita. This is my shop. Can I help you?"

"I need something for a funeral. For Wendy Marx," she said. "Something like what you're putting together here would work, I think. I hate funeral flowers. They always seem so formal and sad."

"Oh, I uh… Are you sure?" the woman asked. "I mean, you are Lilah Ryan, aren't you? Eleanor Barrington Holmes's niece?"

"Cousin, actually, but yes, I'm Lilah." The florist knew her?

"I thought so. I've done a few weddings at the Barrington estate since you came to town and thought that was you. Judge Ashford was in earlier and sent an arrangement to the Marx girl's funeral."

"Yes?" And that meant…what?

The florist just smiled. "He put your name and his on the card that will go with the arrangement, which is right here."

The palest pink and lavender roses. Lilah felt her eyes flush with tears. "They're lovely. Perfect for a young girl. Thank you."

"He came in himself, never does that," the woman said. "Seemed like he wanted to pick out something himself, that it was important to get it just right."

"And he did," Lilah agreed, puzzled.

She could sense the woman was trying to tell her something, but couldn't figure out what, exactly. That Ashe sent flowers all the time to all sorts of women? Lilah wasn't surprised by that.

They just looked at each other for a moment, and then Anita said, "I'm sorry. I just hardly ever go out on deliveries anymore myself, so I never get to see people's faces when they see the flower arrangements I make for them. He sent you flowers, too."

"Oh." Okay, now she got it, feeling a rush of surprise. *Nice touch, Ashe.*

Or was that some kind of standard procedure?

"He picked them out himself," Anita said.

And he didn't normally do that. That's what the woman wanted Lilah to know. It had seemed important to him to get it just right. She felt a little rush of pleasure at the thought.

"I'm sorry. I really want to see your face," Anita said, going back to the arrangement she'd been working on when Lilah arrived. "This is what he picked out for you."

Lilah stared, her mouth falling open. "Oh."

They were absolutely perfect, and they were completely her. All those pretty colors and vibrant green leaves and stems, delicate and a little bit wild.

Ashe saw her.

He understood her.

He'd been paying attention.

It touched something deep inside her, leaving her ridiculously pleased. She smiled, blinking back a few tears. It was an emotional day.

"Here's the card."

She struggled to get the tiny envelope open, because her hands were shaking, and the card had actually been sealed. On the card and in handwriting as bold and sure as the man, she read, *They reminded me of you. —Ashe*

"Well," Lilah said, taking a breath. "Thank you. They're perfect."

Ashe didn't intend to do it, but at the last minute, he went to the cemetery for Wendy Marx's funeral. There was a huge crowd, and he stayed in the back, hoping to go unnoticed by her parents. He was afraid they might still be angry that he'd pushed them into letting the girl go home or maybe that they'd lost her so fast after she'd stopped treatment.

He felt that he should be there but really didn't want to be. In fact, he hoped to simply stand there and try to block everything around him from his mind. Which seemed to make the whole act moot. He certainly wasn't here for appearances' sake. So what was he doing?

A million different emotions swirled through him, churning up his insides, trying to get out. Keeping them in required so much energy of late, it was all he could do to manage it.

Then, through the crowd in front of him, he saw Lilah quietly making her way to him.

He took a breath and held on to it as long as he could, bracing himself for reasons he couldn't understand. She looked sad and already a bit teary-eyed and so beautiful in a long, flowing black-and-white print dress, a little black belt and a little black jacket over it, her hair long and loose. This was as sad as she could look, he thought, sad but still her, still hopeful and kind.

She should never look truly sad, he decided. It just wasn't her.

She came to his side, gave him a kindhearted, understanding smile and then slipped her hand into his and just stood there, holding his hand the whole time. He couldn't believe how much better he felt, just having her hold his hand.

Oh, he still felt like he was practically choking, trying to keep all those swirling emotions inside, to not make a sound or any outward show of anything going on inside of him. But he wasn't alone, and he knew it, because her small, delicate hand was tucked firmly into his, her body brushing ever so slightly against his side, tears falling down her face, her breath coming in shuddering waves at times as she, too, tried to hold her emotions in.

He was glad she was crying, glad she allowed herself that kind of release, and yet it was hard not to simply take her into his arms and hold her close and beg her to stop. She just tangled him up inside in ways in which he was not comfortable.

He held on tighter, and she leaned her head against his arm. The service seemed as if it would never end, and people were weeping openly. It was a hideous thing, to bury someone so young.

Just when he thought he couldn't stand it any longer,

the service ended. The people up front in chairs got to their feet. Those in back who had been standing the whole time started whispering amongst themselves and walking toward their cars.

Lilah remained at his side, still holding on to his arm, the top of her head still resting lightly against him. "Thank you for sending flowers from both of us."

He frowned. "How did you know that?"

"I tried to use the same florist you did, to send flowers of my own. I guess the florist thought you and I had gotten our wires crossed, and I didn't realize you already sent an arrangement from the two of us. I saw the flowers at her shop. The arrangement was lovely."

"The florist said every young girl dreams that one day a boy will send her roses. Do you think anyone ever sent Wendy roses before today?"

Which, he realized too late, was absolutely the wrong thing to say, because Lilah gave a little sob, turned her head away and stared at the ground. He'd made her cry again.

Ashe swore softly, put his arms around her and pulled her close, despite where they were and all the people still milling around. It seemed so many didn't know what to do, not wanting to leave, not knowing what to say, or how to deal with their feelings.

He closed his eyes. With one hand around Lilah's back, one hand tangled in her hair, his chin resting on the top of her head, he wished he could absorb her tears, take every bit of sadness away for her.

Her body felt so slight against his. She was trembling, and he slid his hand to the side of her face and tried to wipe away her tears with his thumb. He was still holding her a minute later when Eleanor made her way to the two of them.

"A terrible day," Eleanor said. "Just terrible."

Lilah sniffled, raised her head and then turned toward Eleanor. "Do we need to leave right now?"

"I do," Eleanor said. "Perhaps the judge can give you a ride home, if you'd like to stay."

"No, that's all right. I'll go with you."

And then Ashe simply couldn't let her leave him. Without even thinking about what he was doing, he reached out and took her hand in his and held on to it. "She'll be fine with me, Eleanor."

Lilah waited until Eleanor was gone, looked down at her hand held in his, then up into his eyes. "I wasn't sure you'd come, and I didn't want to come by myself. But I was afraid I'd be overstepping if I called and asked you to come with me."

"I didn't want to come," he admitted. "I didn't intend to, but then at the last minute I felt like I had to be here."

"You made a difference in her life, Ashe. You know that, don't you? You gave her what she wanted, when no one else would. Let it go. It's done. She's gone, and you did the right thing. I'm sure you almost always do the right thing."

"Not last night, I didn't," he said, sounding more angry than he intended.

Her eyes came up, her gaze locking on to his. Hurt flashed across her pretty face. She pulled her hand from his, turned and started walking away.

He swore under his breath, so angry at himself and everything in the world at the moment. Then he took off after her. "Lilah, wait. I didn't mean it."

She whirled around to face him briefly. "Oh, yes, you did. And I swore to myself I wasn't going to get upset, whatever you said about last night. If we weren't standing at this damned funeral, I wouldn't be, but I'm a little too emotional today."

Then she turned around and kept on walking. He caught up with her, took her by the arm and, with some amount of effort, steered her to his car. He unlocked it, opened the passenger side door and stared down at her, still holding her by the arm.

"Please, get in."

She looked up at him just for a moment, then went back to staring at the ground. "Look, you don't have to explain. I was afraid you'd feel this way, and it's okay. I know you didn't want that to happen—"

"Oh, hell. You know I wanted you as much as you wanted me. I didn't want to want you, but I can't seem to help myself, and you know it."

She just stared up at him, looking both stubborn and hurt.

"Lilah, please get in the car. Please."

And finally, she did.

Now he just had to figure out what he was going to say to her once he got her to his house.

## Chapter Thirteen

Lilah willed herself to be as calm as possible. This was exactly what she did not want to happen, some kind of overwrought scene. She knew it was the last thing he wanted, too.

He drove right past Eleanor's house and she let him. If they had to talk, they should at least do it in private. A few minutes later, they walked into his house, through the kitchen, and then stood awkwardly in the living room, which happened to have huge windows looking onto the patio.

Lilah allowed herself one quick glance at the outdoor sofa, picturing them there together the night before, and felt heat rising in her cheeks. Ashe did the same and looked positively grim.

"I'm sorry," he began.

"Truly, you don't have to say that. I wish you didn't even feel like you needed to say it."

He threw his hands up into the air in frustration. "Of course, I need to say it—"

"Ashe, I'm telling you, you don't. Obviously, you regret it. Obviously, it's not what you wanted to happen. You made that absolutely clear, and I shouldn't have—"

"You didn't. It was me. I did it. All you did was come over here," he insisted.

"And I shouldn't have done that. My mistake."

"No, it was mine. You were just so sad, and I couldn't stand to see you so sad. I just wanted to make you stop crying, that's all. And then…well, you know what happened then."

"I do, and I'm telling you, we don't have to talk about it. I know how you feel. We don't have to talk about anything."

And then she waited, watching him as he watched her, looking wary and serious and sad. What a horrible, horrible day. And all of this was so unnecessary, just making it worse. Lilah walked over to him and dared to put her hands flat against his chest, bracing herself as she stretched up on her tiptoes and kissed his cheek.

"I hate seeing you look so sad, too," she said.

Dark stormy eyes blazed down into hers, as if he wanted her anywhere but there, touching him. But he was bluffing. She still had her hands pressed against his chest, could feel the stillness come over him, the surprise, confusion even.

"What are you doing?" he asked finally.

Offering him just a little bit of comfort, she'd thought at first. A little kiss, her hands on him for just a minute. But from the way he'd reacted, hope surged within her, and then guilt that she should be so happy, when she'd come over here because that poor girl had just died. But she and Ashe were alive and sad and alone, and people did things when they were sad and alone that they might not do otherwise. Was that really so hard to understand? Or so awful?

"I'm doing what I want to do instead of having some silly argument with you."

"I think you love to argue with me," he countered.

"Maybe. But we don't have to. Not now." She leaned into him just a bit more, nestling her head against his chest to help him along a bit.

He caught her hard by her arms, as if to keep her away. "Lilah—"

"I'm telling you that you can have anything you want from me today. You don't have to explain. You don't have to mean it later. I came here last night because I wanted to be with you, in any way at all that might make this a little easier for you, and I want the same thing right now."

"Damn, Lilah. You don't say things like that to a man."

"I'm not saying it to just any man. I'm saying it to you." She was offering herself to him again, with no promises, no expectations, nothing.

He backed her up against the wall, his big, hard body pressed against her.

"You don't mean it," he told her.

"I do. It was just a bad night, Ashe. And today's a bad day. That's all. I understand that. Surely you do, too." It was the best argument she could think of that might get her back in his bed, and she wanted to be back in his bed. Plus, it had the advantage of being true.

She felt fresh tears well up in her eyes, hating that in this moment, not wanting him to think she was trying to manipulate him. Honestly, she wasn't. It was all just so sad. He swore when he saw her tears, cupped her face in his hands and backed off of the hold he had on her with the press of his body.

"Don't do that. Please, don't do that."

She shook her head. "They're just tears. I get sad, and I cry, and then I'm done. It'll be over in a minute. Just... it just doesn't matter that much, Ashe."

"It matters to me," he said, his voice low and rough. "I don't want you to ever feel this way."

She smiled up at him. "I don't think even you, as determined and perfect and powerful as you are, can make sure a woman's happy all the time. But it's a very sweet idea."

"Sweet? I am not sweet." He scowled, looking like a man at war with himself, more uncomfortable with every passing moment.

He leaned down and kissed her once, then again. Long, deep kisses that were like a drug, leaving her weak and clinging to him. Her breasts were suddenly heavy and tingly against his chest, her whole body starting to throb with anticipation and need, her legs shaky.

He lifted her up into his arms and carried her to his bed.

"I have lost my mind," Ashe told Wyatt during a break from court the next morning.

Wyatt didn't look overly concerned. "Lilah? Still?"

"Yes, Lilah. Nothing else makes me crazy. Nobody else."

"Okay, let me point out the obvious, just in case you haven't figured it out yet. If you're not going to actually take the woman to bed and you're not going to see anyone else, she's still going to make you crazy. You either have to find someone else or get on with things with her."

"I did," Ashe admitted, though he wasn't one to bed a woman and brag about it to anyone.

"Did what? Find someone else?" Wyatt asked.

"No. No one else. Lilah. She might still be asleep in my bed right now."

"Oh." Wyatt frowned. "Well, if you're sleeping with her, what the hell's wrong? You should be happy."

"I shouldn't be sleeping with her at all. I didn't mean to. I'd made up my mind, but I just couldn't resist. I wasn't... I just meant... I didn't mean to do it, okay? And you would think, I could just stop, but now... I don't know. It's like I—"

"Can't get enough?" Wyatt suggested.

"And not for lack of trying." Ashe kept trying to tell himself it couldn't be that bad. "It's only been two days. Or...two nights, actually."

Two nights and one really nice morning.

"Just keep trying to get her out of your system," Wyatt advised.

"Really?" Because Ashe was thinking more in terms of exercising a little self-discipline. Surely he could manage that.

"Yeah. That's the only way to go here. Go at it like bunnies until—"

"It's not like that with her," Ashe insisted sharply, angry now that his friend had even implied it might be.

"Really?" Wyatt seemed genuinely surprised. "What is it like?"

"God, I don't know."

"Because I thought you just wanted her in your bed, nothing else. That she was just some gorgeous, sexy complication, who showed up in your life at absolutely the wrong time."

"No question, she is that." Gorgeous, sexy and complicated. And the timing was abysmal. No doubt about it.

"But?" Wyatt prompted.

"She's interesting. She's...always a challenge. She

likes to push me…just outside my comfort zone, and she's really smart, dedicated, almost blindly idealistic at times. Softhearted, kind, fun… That thing she did for Wendy Marx, the girl whose petition I heard, who wanted the right to make her own medical decisions?"

"Yeah, saw the story in the newspaper yesterday. Tough, huh?"

Ashe nodded.

"You should know, in one of the photos of the crowd at the funeral? You and Lilah."

"Really?" Ashe hadn't known that. "Doing…what?"

"Nothing that looks improper. She's obviously upset, and you're standing side by side. I mean, it looks like you're obviously friends, maybe more, attending a funeral together," Wyatt said. "So what did Lilah do for Wendy Marx?"

"A photo shoot. Made her look great—clothes, makeup, hair, lighting, the whole bit. Made her look…pretty and normal, something Wendy really wanted, even if it was just for a photo."

"The one that was in the paper, too?"

"I don't know. Somehow I never even looked at the paper yesterday," Ashe admitted.

"She didn't look sick at all. Outside, smiling, laughing…now that I think of it, was she by that shrub on Eleanor's patio that turns bright red this time of year?"

Ashe nodded. "They did the shoot in Eleanor's backyard."

"I recognize the spot now. Wow. Lilah made her look like a perfectly normal, happy teenage girl." Wyatt shook his head. "I bet that meant a lot to her."

"And Wendy's parents, now that she's gone."

"Okay, so Lilah's a nice but very complicated woman," Wyatt agreed.

Ashe nodded.

"I told you before, you don't have to be a saint to get elected. You just can't look like a jerk where women are concerned or like you're into anything…weird or kinky or outrageous. That's all. You just have to decide if you really want this woman in your life for a while, complications and all."

She was that.

As to wanting her in his life for a while? He certainly couldn't imagine wanting her gone, actually wanting to be without her.

"You're a smart man. You'll figure it out, I swear," Wyatt said.

So why did Ashe feel so uneasy?

Lilah slept late once again, luxuriating in that all-over lazy, happy feeling that came from being here in Ashe's big bed, pleasantly worn out and relaxed as could be after what he'd done to her.

She hoped he didn't regret it as much this morning, as he obviously had yesterday, hoped he wasn't going to show up and apologize again and again, and that she wouldn't have to convince him that they hadn't done anything wrong, nor should they stop doing it.

Smiling happily, she looked around the room, seeing that it was ridiculously late in the morning to still be in bed. He'd left the robe at the end of the bed for her again, her clothes and shoes neatly folded in the bathroom. She took her time getting dressed then went downstairs, turned off the coffee he'd left warming for her and rinsed the coffeepot.

No note this morning, she realized.

And she didn't have her car. She'd forgotten about that until just now.

So, she could call a taxi, Eleanor or...Sybil, she decided. She needed womanly advice, from someone who wasn't eighty-something, someone who'd been out in the dating scene with a man from Ashe's generation recently.

She called, and Sybil was happy to come get her for an early lunch, especially when she told Sybil where she was. Twenty minutes later, Sybil picked her up in a little red sports car, positively beaming at Lilah as she came out of Ashe's house.

"So, he finally gave in," Sybil said. "Good for you."

Lilah couldn't help it. She blushed like crazy.

"And it seems the judge is everything they say he is," Sybil said, zipping around in his driveway and roaring down the road toward town.

Lilah hesitated. Did women really kiss and tell like this? She supposed some of them must. And even if they didn't, Sybil had likely figured out all she needed to know simply from the look on Lilah's face.

"Really? That good?" Sybil said.

Lilah nodded. "But you have to help me. I don't know what to do now. And we have to go somewhere really quiet and out of the way for lunch, because I can't show up anywhere downtown in the same clothes I wore to the funeral yesterday. That would be in really poor taste."

"Okay. I know just the spot."

She did, and minutes later they were seated in a little out-of-the-way bar and grill on the outskirts of town. Lilah was ravenous, ordering a huge lunch, which again had Sybil studying her.

"Worked off that many calories? Really?" she asked.

"We didn't have dinner last night," Lilah admitted.

"Oh, spent the whole evening in bed? How deliciously decadent of you."

Yes, it had been.

"You have to help me, Sybil. I just don't know what to do. It was just so good. I mean, I don't have a lot to compare this to. I married young and just got divorced. But t's... It's just so good. I never want it to end."

"Oh, my." Sybil's eyes got big and round. "After only one night?"

"Two," Lilah admitted.

"Last night and—"

"The night before. But he was mad at himself for the first night, and he kept apologizing, saying it shouldn't have happened at all—"

"And went right back and did it again last night?"

Lilah nodded. "And this morning."

Sybil groaned appreciatively.

"But I don't know what the rules are. Do I stay away and not call him?"

"The rules are whatever you agreed to before this happened," Sybil told her. "If you didn't agree to anything, then it's just sex, unless you both agree that it's more than that now. You need to be careful. If you have all these expectations about what it means to him, you're just going to end up getting hurt."

"We didn't agree to anything, except that I was willing, and he thought it would be a mistake." Lilah sighed. No, wait. Last night, I told him...well, that it could just be that night, nothing more."

"Oh." Sybil looked sorry for her then.

"But...I want more. I want him. What do I do?"

"I think you have to wait for him to come to you now."

"What if he doesn't? I mean, I don't want to be one of those half-crazy stalker women who just won't leave him alone."

"No, you don't," Sybil told her. "And you really can't stalk a judge."

Lilah felt exhausted all of a sudden. "I just don't have any frame of reference here. The last time I had a boyfriend, I was a teenager."

"Oh, my. You really don't know what you're doing."

Maybe it was that good between Ashe and every woman he was with. Maybe there was nothing special about what happened between them.

Was that even possible?

He was so very sexy. Lilah's whole body started tingling just thinking about him. But he was so much more than that. He was good, kind, strong, reliable, responsible. Annoying, argumentative, stubborn, but adorable, too.

"Wait and see what he does," Sybil advised. "If it was that good, he's not going to give it up. I don't care if he thinks it was a mistake or not. Men don't give up on something that good. Unless the woman's flat-out loony and a ton of trouble."

"He thinks I'm a lot of trouble," Lilah said sadly. "Or that I will be. That it's too soon for me to know what I want after my divorce, and he has these rules about recently divorced women, and he's nuts about following his own rules."

"Well, he's already broken one of his precious rules with you. No reason he can't break some more," Sybil suggested.

Lilah closed her eyes and thought about the worst thing, the scariest thing. "What if I really fall for him? What if... I think, I might already love him?"

"Oh, don't," Sybil said. "Please, for your own sake, don't do that."

Lilah didn't say any more. She couldn't. Didn't even want to give voice to what she already knew in her ridiculous heart.

It was already too late.

\* \* \*

Ashe debated with himself on every break in court. He could call her, but maybe he shouldn't. He could send flowers in place of calling, but he'd just sent flowers the day before so he wouldn't have to call. He couldn't really send flowers two days in a row. Although she'd clearly been pleased with the first arrangement.

He could ignore her, for as long as he could make that last, but that would make him feel both rude and like a jerk. He really wasn't a jerk.

Or he could go see her, haul her back into his bed and wake up tomorrow facing this same dilemma. The only plus was that he'd have her back in his bed once again and could do his absolute best to have so much of her, he might start to get over her at some point, maybe in the next year? Next decade? Much as he loved Wyatt's plan, Ashe just didn't see it as a viable answer. Not any time soon, at least.

And then, he realized he'd never even taken the woman to dinner, nothing remotely like a date. That first lunch didn't count. It had been purely for business reasons. What kind of man bedded a woman repeatedly and never even took her to dinner? That made him sound both rude and a like a jerk, which ended up being his excuse.

He called and asked her to have dinner with him that evening.

There. He'd get to see her, and there would be people around, so there was some hope they could both keep their clothes on for a while, at least.

It was only later that it occurred to him that while he would get to see her, he'd also have to talk to her. Which meant, he also had to figure out what to say to her.

*Damn.*

## Chapter Fourteen

Lilah fully expected to get dumped over dinner.

The man had too much time to think, and he'd regretted every time they'd ended up in his bed together. So what else could she expect him to say? But she didn't have to make it easy for him.

She was trying every relaxation method she'd ever learned in all her years at school to stay calm, thinking about him breaking her heart, just when she'd plastered it back together again after her divorce. And she took special care to pull out her favorite perfume, one she made herself from a blend of essential oils, piled her hair on top of her head, found a rather plain, long, shiny black silk skirt that she paired with a dressy, cream-colored halter top with extra-long, wide ties that wrapped around her waist several times, leaving her arms and much of her back bare. She put long, dangly lines of diamonds in her ears and wrapped a black lace shawl around her shoulders.

There, she was ready. If he was going to give her up, she wanted him to know what he'd be losing. She'd be fine without him. She had Eleanor, Kathleen, Gladdy, Sybil, her students and work she loved. She could think about the series of classes she wanted to offer next. She was almost finished with the current ones, almost time for that divorce ceremony, which she didn't think she had a prayer of getting Ashe to perform. Hard to believe that all of this between them had started with that one simple thing, one request—and Kathleen, Gladdy and Eleanor's meddling, of course.

Lilah also wanted to spend some extra time with Erica, who was really scared of what her husband would do when their divorce was finally granted, which was supposed to happen very soon. If things stayed as tense as they were now, Lilah was leaning toward recommending that Erica disappear for a few weeks after the divorce, just to be safe.

And then there was Sybil. The two of them were talking about other ways in which their two businesses could work together. They had all sorts of ideas about joint ventures. So Lilah was a woman with things to do. She'd survive this, wouldn't she?

Ashe arrived promptly at the appointed time, looking as polished and serious as ever, polite as could be, the perfect escort. He was taking her to the nicest restaurant in town, or at least one of them, judging by the decor, and a very popular one, judging by the crowd, where he appeared to be well-known. The maitre d' greeted him by name, as did several people who shook his hand. He introduced her to each and every one of them as more than a few eyebrows arched in surprise.

So, no more hiding her?

That was unexpected.

Lilah didn't quite know what to make of it.

True, they hadn't had any disasters of late that involved them almost getting caught together in various embraces or stages of undress. But Ashe's boss was still watching him closely, and there had been a small photo of them together in the crowd at Wendy's funeral that had shown up in the newspaper. Nothing improper, but together—two people caught up in grief, but obviously very close.

Lilah looked up at Ashe.

If she hadn't known better, she would have thought the man was nervous. About dumping her? Why? He'd probably done it often enough. Maybe he even had a checklist for it.

Although she had to admit this seemed an odd choice of restaurants for the end of a relationship, if what they had would even qualify as that.

For spite, maybe, or just to rattle him, she let the shawl drop from her shoulders as they got to the table and Ashe stepped up to pull out her chair before the maitre d' could.

He didn't touch her, just held her chair, but she could tell the moment he spotted her bare back. She felt him go still, could swear she felt his eyes on her bare skin, taking it all in. He cleared his throat, pushed her chair up to the table and then sat down, looking positively grim.

"Oh, stop it," she said, fed up with both of them. "I told you, you don't have to do this—"

"What? Feed you? At least every now and then? I've hustled you off to bed two nights in a row without dinner, and I'm out the door in the morning, leaving you with nothing but coffee and...I don't know, maybe some crackers if you rifled through the cabinets."

Lilah was taken aback. "We're here because you feel guilty about not feeding me?"

"I wouldn't call it guilt, exactly. More like...?"

"What? Good manners?" She laughed, seeing by his reaction she was close enough. "I don't think Miss Manners has a guide to what's considered polite when two people have done nothing but share a bed for two nights, Ashe. You don't have to worry."

"Well, I do," he claimed.

"Oh. So, the women you're sleeping with normally get dinner first? One of your little rules?" He bedded them, but he was polite about it? Why would that infuriate her?

"Why did you think we were here?" he asked.

"So you could dump me in a classy way," she admitted.

"Why?" Now he seemed completely perplexed.

"Look, you don't have to worry. We didn't make each other any promises, and I'm not expecting any. I'm not going to give you a hard time or cause some kind of scene. You want this to stop, it stops."

"Why are you so sure I want this to stop?"

"Because you've been so uncomfortable with the whole thing." It was so obvious. He couldn't deny it.

He sat back in his chair, looked her up and down very slowly. "It surprised me. It wasn't what I intended—"

"Oh, I know that."

"But much as I've tried, I haven't quite been able to bring myself to the point of regretting it," he claimed.

"Really?" she said, challenging him.

He shrugged. "At least not for any real period of time. I know I should. I tell myself I should. I believe it for maybe three seconds, and then I'm thinking about getting you naked again and how sexy you look sleeping practically sideways in my bed with the covers off and a sheet draped over maybe half of you. You sleep like a wild woman. All over the place. All over me. Not that I'm complaining."

Lilah's heart kicked into high gear, relief and anticipation zinging through her. Finally, quietly, she told him, "I think that's maybe the most honest thing you've ever said to me."

He laughed. "Might be the most honest thing I've ever said to anybody. Except when we talked about Wendy. That was honest. It wasn't…the kind of conversation I normally allow myself to have. And I shouldn't have done it, but it was nice. It helped."

"You should have someone to talk to about things like that. We all need people we can talk to, people who care."

"And make us a little bit crazy?"

Okay, her heart was really pounding at that. He still looked surprised and puzzled, but so perfect to her. "You, especially, need someone like that."

He grinned. "It's funny you'd say that, because I talked to Wyatt today. I shouldn't have, and I don't want you to think I go around talking about things like this with just anyone—"

"Ashe, I know that."

"So, I told him I thought I should just stay away from you, but I can't even make that last a day," he admitted, shaking his head and staring at her with a sexy, simmering fire in his eyes.

"What did Wyatt say?"

"Well…I'm sorry, but there's no way to say this without sounding like a jerk—"

"To get everything you could, while you could?" she guessed.

He nodded.

"Until you get tired of me and move on?"

"Yes," he admitted.

"Sounds like something Wyatt would say." Not that she objected to that plan, because if nothing else, it meant more time with Ashe, and who knew what could happen eventually if she had more time with Ashe? So she just went ahead and said it. "Go ahead. Try to get tired of me. I dare you."

Ashe looked surprised, then just plain annoyed. "You don't mean that—"

"Why not?"

"Because you're not that kind of woman."

Before he could say anything more, their waiter arrived. They ordered a bottle of wine and both decided on one of the dinner specials the waiter rattled off. Then finally they were alone again.

"Don't tell me what kind of woman I am or what I want," she told him, knowing he was about to do that very thing. "We're not in your courtroom. You don't get to make all the decisions here."

"Lilah, you were married to the same man and completely faithful to him for ten years."

"And now I'm not—"

"I know what kind of woman you are, and I think it's time we stop pretending this is just about sex."

Lilah's mouth dropped open, literally.

"We tried to make it that, but it's not," he insisted. "You know that, and I know it. I don't go to this much trouble for just sex. I don't have to."

"This much trouble?"

"For a relationship that's nothing but sex? No, I don't. Sex is simple. Why wouldn't it be? It's just sex. But you and I are more than that. Can we just…get that out there on the table?"

"Well, this doesn't have to be that much trouble for you," she told him. "You can just go have simple, nothing-but-sex with someone else."

"I don't want to, Lilah. Apparently I want something

complicated and…I don't even know what else. But whatever it is, I want it with you. Just you."

"Oh." She sat back in her chair, all the fight going out of her, all the breath, it seemed. *Just you.* "Oh…well. But I thought—"

"So did I, but either I was wrong in the first place, or I changed my mind. You're…a very interesting, complicated woman, and…I like you. I want you. In and out of bed."

"Oh," she said, as if her vocabulary had shrunk to nearly nothing.

"You could say you feel the same way," he prompted, when she said nothing else for a long moment.

"I do," she managed.

"Good."

"Good." She had to remind herself to breathe, and her head was spinning.

He liked her. He wanted her.

Such simple words from a very complicated man. Words that thrilled her, pleased her immensely, excited her, scared her a little, because of how much she'd found she wanted to hear that from him and how much she trusted him when he said it, despite all she'd been through.

It was a different life, she told herself, a different man, a better man, and she was a different woman.

"Don't get scared now," he said, laughing. "You're the one who's been fearless the whole time."

"All right, I'm not. But you had so many reservations about this. What about those? What about your election?"

"What about it? I'm not going to ask you to change for me, if that's what you're worried about. I wouldn't do that to you."

"Really? Because, I thought—"

"Because I like you the way you are. So besides the fact that it would be hypocritical, I wouldn't hurt you that way," he said.

"Ashe..." It was so sweet, she almost cried.

"Well..." He smiled. "Maybe if we could just keep our clothes on, everywhere except in private? Although I think I've been guiltier than you on that count."

She nodded. Could this really be happening? "I'm willing to do my part, if you'll do yours."

"Well, there you go."

"No, you know it's not that simple. I know how important your job is to you, and I happen to believe you're really good at it. You should be on the bench, and I don't want to do anything to mess that up for you."

"Thank you," he said sincerely. "Maybe this won't be as difficult as we thought."

Ashe had to admit in the weeks that followed that he was a happy man, and despite his initial misgivings, he found it so easy with her.

She was a happy woman, enthusiastic about her work and doing something she thought was important. She found Eleanor and her friends delightful, despite their outrageous, meddling ways. And honestly, Ashe enjoyed them, too, when he wasn't worried about what they might say or do to harm his reelection efforts.

Then there was Sybil. She and Lilah were becoming good friends, something that freaked Ashe out a little bit because of how well-known Sybil was around town. But the benefit was, Lilah was often at Sybil's store and brought things home to wear for him. He didn't think he could be such a hypocrite as to enjoy seeing Lilah in everything she brought home from Sybil's store and still disapprove of Sybil. He wasn't that much of a politician. But it worried him.

She was really, really smart, kind, beautiful and, in bed, enthusiastic, adventurous and utterly delightful. She'd worn that little flesh-colored slip the other night, the one she'd teased him with that day of the fundraiser, and he'd just about gone insane, ending up laying her across his desk at the house like a meal he intended to devour. Which was pretty much what he'd done.

If Ashe didn't know better, he'd say she was a perfect woman. But no woman was perfect. No man was. No relationship was. He believed this with absolute conviction.

So, she was a puzzle.

Too good to be true.

Life, at the moment, seemed too good to be true.

Oh, there were minor hassles. He really had to get moving on his reelection effort, which he expected to be pure aggravation. His caseload was too high, but it always was. And he hadn't had a woman in his house every night since his brief marriage nearly fifteen years ago, which took some getting used to, but also meant Lilah was in his bed every night, and he wanted her in his bed every night.

There was a new threat against him from a disgruntled, now ex-husband who thought he'd gotten a raw deal in Ashe's courtroom, but that was just part of the job. It happened. He'd have a little extra security for a few days until the police could find the man and decide whether he was a real risk.

Which meant he'd have to tell Lilah.

He'd do it in bed, he decided, distract her, make it sound like nothing, which it likely was. He didn't want her to worry. In fact, he'd be happy if everything just kept going exactly as it was.

When was the last time he could say that about his life?

And then, early that evening, as he was working late knowing Lilah had a class until eight-thirty, one of the cops on his newly assigned security detail walked into Ashe's office with a look on his face that nearly brought Ashe to his knees. He knew. Somehow, he just knew something terrible was coming.

"What happened?"

"We think we found the man who threatened you. Joe Reynolds?"

"Reynolds? Where?"

"The Barrington estate—"

Ashe went cold. It was an effort just to speak. "Lilah. She's my… The woman I'm…" *Crazy about. Can't get enough of. Am so happy with.* "The woman I'm seeing." That description seemed completely inadequate. He had to fight the urge to simply say *My woman.*

"What about her?" the officer asked.

"She lives there. Works there. Is she okay?"

"We don't have any reports of injuries so far, but… from what I've heard on the radio, we have to be careful how we approach this guy."

Approach? What did he mean by that?

*Oh, my God,* Ashe realized. "He has hostages?"

"I don't know. We had a 911 call. A man stormed into the house looking for his wife. When he didn't find her inside, he spotted a campfire in the backyard and went to look for her there."

Ashe nodded. "Lilah has class tonight. A dozen women, all newly separated or divorced."

"Yeah, class around a campfire? What is that about?"

"It's not important now," Ashe insisted. "What is important is that Lilah's had a woman in one of her classes who was scared of her ex-husband. Ah, dammit. We must have been dealing with the same couple, the same man."

He hadn't even told her about the threat yet. He'd tried the other night, but the threat had been anonymous. He didn't even have a name to mention to Lilah. And their jobs were just too entwined. It was a small town, and they both dealt with people going through divorces. So they made a point not to talk about any specific cases with each other. Which meant he'd been forced to settle for asking if any of the women in her classes had a husband or an ex who was violent or seemed to have the potential to turn violent. She'd said she didn't, but he could tell there was at least one person who was worrying her in some way. He'd asked her to promise to be careful, and had let it go at that.

God, what had he done?

"Come on," Ashe told the man. "I'm going—"

"Judge, I can't let you do that."

"I'm going. You can come with me or you can follow me. I don't care which one."

Ashe made it to his car, the cop on his tail, at the last minute getting in the car with Ashe, trying all the way to talk him out of going to the scene or at least into moving a little more slowly. The drive, ten minutes at most, seemed interminable. He saw flashing blue lights, a lot of them, then all the police cars. Ashe cut the engine, was out and striding down the driveway when the cop who'd ridden with him literally grabbed him and swung him around.

"I can't let you charge into the middle of this, Judge—"

"He wants me. I'm the one who granted the divorce. I'll tell him I can undo it. I'll un-divorce him."

He got a really weird look from the cop at that. Undivorce? He could do that ceremony Lilah had wanted from the start, except in reverse. The un-divorce.

"No," the cop said. "We are not giving anybody a judge as a hostage—"

But Ashe had jerked his arm free and was heading for the house, for whoever was in charge. The guy said in his threat that he wanted Ashe, and Ashe was going to make sure the guy got him. Simple as that.

And Lilah would be safe.

But nothing he said would convince the cops in charge that his plan would work. They kept asking what Lilah and her class could be doing back there around the camp-fire, and there was no way he was up to explaining that she liked the full moon and rituals and burning things for the symbolism of letting go of crap. He couldn't explain that to a bunch of cops, and it didn't matter anyway.

Then one of the cops asked, "Is it possible that all those women are wearing wedding gowns? Really ratty, torn, messed-up wedding gowns? God, what did the guy do to them?"

Ashe groaned, remembering then that it was destroy-the-dress night or something like that, the one Lilah had warned him about the first time they'd met. And now the cops were looking at him for an explanation.

"There's a man with a gun back there," he yelled. "How can it possibly matter what the hostages are wear-ing?"

"Okay. Sorry, Judge."

"Look, I think I remember this man. I granted his wife a restraining order against him, and I'm the one who can revoke that order. That's what he wants. To be able to see and talk to his wife again," Ashe said, trying to sound as reasonable as possible, when it was the absolute last thing he was feeling. "Tell him I'm here, that I think I may have been unfair to him before and that I'm willing to grant him an emergency hearing, right now, on revoking the restraining order, provided he lets everyone else go."

"We're not giving him a judge," the incident commander repeated.

"I'm part of the law enforcement community. I knew the risks when I took this job," Ashe insisted. "Better me than a dozen innocent women, which is what he's got right now—"

"The chief of police would have my head—"

"You know it's much easier for you to protect one person than a dozen. Offer him the deal. Tell him we'll set up a courtroom out there in the backyard. No, tell him the hearing isn't legal unless a court reporter's present to make a transcript of the proceedings. That she has to have an electrical outlet to plug in her equipment, so we have to hold the hearing in the house. You can have the room surrounded before he ever walks into it. All I'll have to do is stand there and wait for him."

Ashe kept talking, being as judicial and authoritative as possible, and finally the incident commander agreed to try it. It took a while, but they got everything set up, including a female officer to impersonate a court reporter. And ultimately the gunman agreed to the plan.

Finally a dozen women in wedding dresses—all in various stages of destruction, whether shredded, muddy, grass-stained or torn—slowly walked from the backyard into the light at the back of the house. And wasn't that an interesting sight to everyone but Ashe.

He ignored the looks and all the questions.

All he wanted was Lilah.

His gaze locked on hers for a long moment, noting that she seemed remarkably calm and composed. There wasn't a mark on her that he could see, so she hadn't been hurt. Thank God. He breathed just a little bit more easily.

But she was also walking arm in arm with a terrified Erica Reynolds, whose husband had a bruising grip on Erica's other arm with one hand and a gun in the other.

Of course that's where Lilah would be. Right beside the woman.

Ashe was seething. They all stood there unmoving. He and the officer impersonating a court reporter were both behind a desk they'd set up in the sunroom, which the cops liked because of all the windows, so they could see into the room at all angles and place their sharpshooters where they wanted.

Lilah took in the mock courtroom setup, Ashe standing there waiting, and he could tell she was mad.

*Well, too damn bad.*

If she was in trouble, he was going to do whatever he could to get her out of it. She might as well get used to that right now. He was mad at her, too, for having a job that put her in contact with women with ex-husbands with guns, who went nuts sometimes.

Finally the other women in Lilah's class were gone. It was just her, Erica and Erica's husband. Ashe had been waiting for Lilah to go, too. But before she did, Erica caught Lilah's arm and shot her a pleading look. Lilah hesitated, looking torn.

*Don't do it. Don't you dare do it. Don't you stay here,* Ashe was practically screaming inside his head.

But she did it.

*Dammit all,* she did it!

"I'll stay with you," she said, looking Erica in the eye.

"No. This is a private matter. A private hearing," Ashe claimed. "Me, the court reporter, this man and his wife. That's it, Lilah."

Reynolds pointed his gun at Lilah. Ashe felt as if someone had literally stopped his heart from beating, as if the world had stopped turning on its axis. Why didn't the cops just shoot him already? It was all Ashe could do not to jump across the desk and put himself between Lilah and that gun.

"Wait a minute," Reynolds said, turning from Lilah to Ashe. "You know her? You two are in this together. To get Erica away from me."

"No, but Lilah and I do know each other. We're involved," Ashe said, "and because of that, it's completely improper for me to preside over a case involving you and your wife. Conflict of interest. I'm sorry. I wasn't aware that Lilah was working with your wife until today, but now that I am, I'm going to invalidate every ruling I've made in your case so far. It's the only fair and legal thing to do. You'll be starting over completely with the divorce proceedings."

"No restraining order?" Reynolds asked.

"No restraining order," Ashe claimed. "Just come inside and let's get this done."

And then Reynolds seemed to crumple before them, shrinking inside himself, overwhelmed with despair. "It won't matter. Not anymore. Not now that I've done this."

He looked down at the gun still in his hand, and it seemed everyone in the room knew he was going to use it—he was going to shoot someone.

And in the blink of an eye, it was over.

The cops ended it. Someone rushed the man from his right side. Then they had him on the ground, disarmed and cuffed. In that brief moment, somehow Ashe got across the room and hauled Lilah into his arms.

It felt as if he was shaking even more than she was, but she was safe, and he had her. He'd never been so relieved in his life.

* * *

It took an eternity to sort things out, for the police to ask their questions, for Lilah to soothe all her clients, for her to deal with Erica and to reassure Eleanor, Kathleen and Gladdy that she was all right.

Ashe refused to leave her side as she did it, glaring at anyone who tried to separate them, and before Ashe could be alone with her, they had to get past the throng of media gathered on the road at the entrance to the estate. They were big news. People just didn't take hostages in their little town. Ashe wanted to barrel past the reporters, but Lilah didn't. Lilah wanted to use this chance to talk about domestic violence.

So he stood beside her for a few moments longer while she talked. She was brilliant, he thought, so passionate, so strong, so committed. Of course, there were reporters who only wanted to know about strange ceremonies around a fire under the full moon and women dressed in demolished wedding dresses, but she handled those beautifully as well, using the opportunity to explain what her classes were about.

Ashe was so proud.

There were questions about their relationship, too, and potential conflicts of interest between his work and hers. He took those questions. Then he finally got to take her home with him and shut out the entire world.

A moment after he got her inside, he had her back in his arms, holding her so hard, he was afraid she could barely breathe.

"I'm okay. I promise," she said over and over again.

Yet he was still completely irrational, heart pounding, lungs heaving as he struggled to get enough air.

Inside his head, he kept telling himself, *She's safe, She's safe, She's safe,* but it wasn't helping. Holding her was, a little bit. He could feel the breath going in and out of her lungs and her heart beating.

"I went nuts when I found out that guy had you," he finally told her.

"Ashe." She eased her head back just enough so that she could look him in the eye, took his face in her hands and said, "Please believe me when I tell you, I am absolutely fine."

Ashe felt as if he were standing on quicksand, as if every surface in his whole world had shifted.

Lilah tried to get him to sit down, but he was too amped up.

She finally pushed him down into an oversize leather chair, then climbed onto his lap and wrapped her arms around him.

"Let's try this instead," she said, very softly pressing her lips to his, kissing him gently, completely unhurriedly. "Better?"

"Yes," he admitted. "Don't let go."

"I wont."

Just like that.

That was Lilah.

He needed, and she gave. So easily, generously, sweetly, extravagantly. What a gift that was.

Wyatt was insane. There was no way to stop wanting a woman like this. Life was so much better with her in it, full of pleasure and wonder and the kind of comfort he had never had before. How she both eased every bit of tension inside him, making him think all was right with the world, and at the same time drove him crazy, he didn't understand. But she did it.

The world filled with a reassuring sense of rightness and an extravagance of pleasure. That's what he'd found with her.

She kissed him sweetly, gently, once again.

"I absolutely adore you," he told her.

"And I adore you right back."

He took it one step further. "I need you. So much it scares me."

"Me, too. To both of those things, Ashe."

"I can't imagine living without you. I don't even want to try." Phew, got that out, too.

"You don't have to," she told him.

And that's when he knew.

No, he'd known earlier that day.

This was the moment when he gave up and stopped fighting it.

*Aw, dammit,* he'd gone and fallen in love with her.

Ashe felt as if he'd awakened in another world, a damned scary one.

He was lying on his back in the middle of the bed, and Lilah, for reasons he'd never understand, had curled around his waist. Her hair was spread out all over his chest, her head on his abdomen, breath rushing over his belly button as she breathed slowly and deeply in her sleep. If she woke up like this, she'd start licking him, which was never really a bad thing.

But he had a lot of things he had to say to a number of people, and he didn't know what any of them were going to say in return. And he really needed to know what certain people were going to say to him today, most importantly, her.

"You're going to starve if you stay with me," he said, stroking a hand through her hair once he felt her stirring beside him.

She rubbed her nose against his skin and then kissed his abdomen. "I don't care."

"I could at least keep something in the house for us to eat for breakfast."

"You're never here for breakfast," she reminded him.

"But you are." He reached for her, pulling her up and into his arms, kissing her softly on her gorgeous lips in return. "I want to take care of you, Lilah. It's what a man does for a woman."

She laughed. "How very old-fashioned of you."

"Yeah." Wait until he tried to tell her the rest of it. And once said, he couldn't take it back. They wouldn't just be able to go back to things being the way they were now. And things were very, very good now.

Except, it wasn't enough.

Yesterday had shown him that so clearly.

He glanced over at the clock and sighed. "I have to go to the courthouse. I'm going to cancel my cases for today, but I still have to go in for a couple of hours. Wait here. Right here. Please."

"You really have to go?"

"I do. I have to apologize for interfering with a police operation, at the very least. And probably explain myself to the administrative judge." This would probably take some groveling, too. There were things expected of a man in his position, and barging past a police barricade and disrupting an ongoing situation was not conduct becoming of a judge.

"What are you going to tell them?" she asked.

"I'll think of something. That's not really my main concern right now," he admitted.

She lifted her head, blinking up at him sleepily. "What is?"

"You. How I'm going to explain it to you," he said, nerves getting the better of him.

Maybe it would be easier if she was half asleep.

She took his face in her hands, smiling easily. "You don't have to explain anything to me."

"Yeah, I do," he said, because he didn't think he could wait any longer to hear what she'd say, even if it did mean he had to tell her exactly how he felt to find out. Life was so strange these days.

"I get it. You were scared. It was kind of sweet."

"Sweet?" he nearly growled. "There was nothing sweet about it. I was flat-out terrified. I couldn't think straight. I acted like a crazy man. The cops looked at me like I'd grown three heads."

"Well, I'm sorry, but—"

"Oh, hell, I'm not mad at you. I'm still…terrified, mostly. And I'm sorry, but I really have to go cancel my cases and pawn off the ones I can't cancel on someone else. Two hours, tops, I swear. Please be here when I get back."

"Okay," she said, sounding impossibly relaxed and sleepy, her body all warm and inviting, cuddled up against his this way.

He stayed there with her until she fell back to sleep, thinking…

*Sweet?*

She thought the way he felt about her was *sweet?*

For such a smart woman, could she be that clueless about his feelings for her? Of course, he thought of himself as a very smart man, and he'd just figured it out himself.

Lilah slept late, figuring that a woman who'd been held at gunpoint deserved to do so. Plus, it always felt so good to be in Ashe's bed, her body warm and pleasantly sated, so relaxed, so happy.

The evening before was something of a blur. Erica's husband waving around that gun. Erica and all the women so scared. But Ashe had been there. He'd offered himself up to Erica's husband in exchange for Lilah and the other women in her class. She'd felt so much better just hearing that he was nearby in the house, but then to hear him suggesting a hearing to Erica's husband to get Lilah and the others away from that man... Even if she'd been mad at Ashe for putting himself in danger, she couldn't help but be stunned by the lengths to which he was prepared to go to get her to safety.

And then, last night, once they were alone...

*I can't imagine living without you. I don't even want to try.*

She shivered, just thinking about it.

And this morning she'd tried to give him an out, saying it was sweet that he was so concerned about her, and he hadn't taken it. Apparently there was nothing sweet about how he felt.

Lilah got up and showered, put on a robe and had just gone into the kitchen for coffee when Sybil called and told her she had to turn on the TV that instant.

She did and found grainy footage of the front of Eleanor's house surrounded by police cars, no doubt caught with a long-range lens as the situation unfolded. The reporter explained the situation, and then there were Lilah and Ashe as they'd finally left.

He looked so intense and serious, had her anchored against his side with an arm around her waist. Reporters shouted questions, and Lilah remembered talking about the dangers of domestic violence and the toll it takes on women's lives, and she knew Ashe had fielded some questions, too, but it had all been a blur to her.

Someone had made a catty comment about Lilah's "weird" class, and he'd jumped in, looking very important and judicial, using his most serious judge's voice, and said, "Her methods may be somewhat unconventional, but the work she does is so important. I can grant couples a legal divorce, but an emotional divorce is a very different thing and every bit as important a part of people healing and moving on with their lives. I see clearly, every day in my courtroom, that the divorce process doesn't end the day a divorce is granted. Most people have a lot of work to do at that point, and Lilah helps them do it. I'm very proud of her and the work she does."

There was more, she knew, a question about Ashe's role in ending the hostage situation. It was something he downplayed, claiming he was surrounded by police the entire time and never in any real danger—the closest thing to a lie she'd ever heard him say. He'd stood there in front of a man with a gun for her. Deliberately put himself there, and anything could have happened.

But the way he'd defended her, praised the work she did as important and said he was proud of her...

Lilah started crying—couldn't help it.

He saw all of that in her, despite the fact that she'd been outrageous to him more than once, because he could be so serious and seem so disapproving, and because she'd wanted him to notice her, wanted to shake him up and make him want her. But he saw through that, too, and saw who she was, and he was proud. She didn't think a man had ever been proud of her before or seen her for who she truly was and understood her.

It meant the world to her.

She was still sitting there, tear tracks on her face, when Ashe got back, looking distressed at the evidence of her tears. He rushed to her side and sat down, pulling her into his arms. "What happened? What's wrong now?"

"Nothing. I was just watching the news report from last night."

"Dammit, what did those idiots say about you? Whatever it is, we'll fix it. Eleanor called this morning. She is your fiercest defender. She's mounting a PR campaign right now. All the TV stations want interviews from anyone inside the house last night, or better yet, back there around the campfire. Eleanor's going to talk to them, and she will sing your praises. So will Erica. She wants to. She said you were amazing, keeping everyone calm, including her ex, last night around the campfire. Eleanor talked to Wendy Marx's mom, too. She wants to tell people what you did for Wendy."

Lilah cried even harder.

"Ah, honey. Don't. Please?" he said. "I'm so sorry. People are idiots. TV reporters, especially—"

"It's not that," she said.

He eased away from her, just far enough to see her face. "Then what is it?"

"You."

He blinked, took a deep breath, looked a little scared. "What did I do? I'll fix it, whatever it is. I swear."

"I just saw a news clip of us as we were leaving the estate. It was…something of a blur to me last night, but I heard it all just a few minutes ago. Everything you said about me. You defended me—"

"Of course I did. I'm always going to defend you," he said, as if there would never be any question about it.

"You said you were proud of me and of the work I do."

"Lilah, how could a man not be proud of you? You're an amazing woman."

"I don't think anyone's ever said anything that meant more to me," she said, sniffling and trying to stop crying.

He thought about that for a moment, and then said, "Well, I might have to try to top that."

"Really?"

He nodded. "You said some of last night was a blur, so I'll say this again. I can't stand the thought of losing you, can't imagine my life without you. Not one single day of it. I want…everything. Absolutely everything, Lilah. With you. That's how I feel. Surprised the hell out of me, before it scared me half to death."

She just looked at him.

"Say something," he begged.

But she didn't. She couldn't, because she was about to cry again.

"Ah, dammit, don't do that. Anything but that," he begged.

"I'm…surprised."

"Well, yeah. I'm sure you are. What else?" he demanded. "Give me a break. I'm dying here."

"I just didn't know if you'd ever say that," she finally managed.

"Lilah, when I found out that man had you, I just lost it. I was scared to death. The cops threatened to handcuff me to the freezer to keep me from charging onto the back lawn at one point. I'd handcuff you to me right now if I had a pair of cuffs. I mean, I know it's really not about a little bit of steel and a lock. We both know that's not what staying together is about, but I'd do it anyway."

"You don't have to handcuff me," she promised him.

"I want it all. Vows. A license. A ring. I want you to share my house. Take my name. Everything. Although

I damned well know, too, that's no guarantee you won't ever leave me. Why I feel like I need it, I don't know, but I do. I need for you to marry me. I don't have a ring. I didn't even think through everything I wanted to say. I just…" All of a sudden he stopped, giving her a puzzled look. "I love you. Did I say that?"

"No, you didn't."

"Dammit, I'm bungling this whole thing."

She laughed. "No, you're not, and I love you, too."

"And you'll marry me?"

"Yes."

He laughed. "Just like that?"

"I told you already, you can have anything you want from me."

"And that's what you meant?" he asked, working really hard to wipe all her tears away. "The whole time?"

"No. Not at first. At first I was just insane from wanting you, knowing it was going to be unlike anything I'd ever felt before, it was so good. And then part of it was me needing to prove to myself that I could make you want me, too."

"No problem there," he said.

"Then I had to fight not to be terrified at how much I wanted you and needed you. I didn't expect this. Not now. Maybe not ever. But there you were… What was I supposed to do? Tell you to go away and come back in a few years? When I might be ready?"

"No, I'm not going anywhere."

"Me, either. I don't want to. I want you. But Ashe… your campaign, the election…I don't want to do anything to hurt your career."

"Lilah, everyone who gets to know you loves you. I'm not saying it's going to be easy. There will be idiots who say hurtful things, to try to hurt you to get to me, and I'm truly sorry for that. But you have so many people ready to stand beside you and defend you. I hate asking you to put up with this—"

"Ashe, I would do anything for you," she promised.

"Me, too. For you. I'm not giving you up, and I happen to think we can do anything, that we can get through anything together. Do you believe that?"

"I do," she said.

"Then it's settled. You're going to marry me?"

"I am." She laughed then. "Eleanor, Kathleen and Gladdy are going to be so happy. They're getting exactly what they wanted."

"Honey, they got what they wanted weeks ago," he reminded her.

"No, they wanted this all along."

"But they said they only wanted me to…initiate you. back into the ways of single womanhood, which was a privilege and pleasure."

"They lied. About everything. Wyatt's wife, Jane, got home yesterday. She told me everything. They fancy themselves as matchmakers extraordinaire. It's their newest hobby. We were manipulated from the start."

"I knew that. I just thought…"

"That they'd settle for us in bed together? No, they want us married."

"Well, then, they're going to be very happy women." And likely a part of Ashe and Lilah's lives for a long time, meddling joyously, outrageously.

"I think I'll ask them to be bridesmaids," Lilah said. "They'd get a kick out of that, and they've been so sweet to me. To us."

Ashe could just imagine it. "They'll hit on every single man over thirty-five at the wedding."

"Or find another very lucky couple's lives to meddle in."

\* \* \* \* \*

# HEART & HOME

Heartwarming romances where love can
happen right when you least expect it.

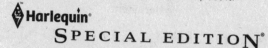

## SPECIAL EDITION®

**COMING NEXT MONTH**
AVAILABLE MAY 29, 2012

### #2191 FORTUNE'S PERFECT MATCH
*The Fortunes of Texas: Whirlwind Romance*
Allison Leigh

### #2192 ONCE UPON A MATCHMAKER
*Matchmaking Mamas*
Marie Ferrarella

### #2193 THE RANCHER'S HIRED FIANCÉE
*Brighton Valley Babies*
Judy Duarte

### #2194 THE CAMDEN COWBOY
*Northbridge Nuptials*
Victoria Pade

### #2195 AN OFFICER, A BABY AND A BRIDE
*The Foster Brothers*
Tracy Madison

### #2196 NO ORDINARY JOE
Michelle Celmer

You can find more information on upcoming Harlequin® titles,
free excerpts and more at www.HarlequinInsideRomance.com.

HSECNM0512

# REQUEST YOUR FREE BOOKS!
## 2 FREE NOVELS PLUS 2 FREE GIFTS!

**❖ Harlequin®**

# SPECIAL EDITION
## Life, Love & Family

**YES!** Please send me 2 FREE Harlequin® Special Edition novels and my 2 FREE gifts (gifts are worth about $10). After receiving them, if I don't wish to receive any more books, I can return the shipping statement marked "cancel." If I don't cancel, I will receive 6 brand-new novels every month and be billed just $4.49 per book in the U.S. or $5.24 per book in Canada. That's a saving of at least 14% off the cover price! It's quite a bargain! Shipping and handling is just 50¢ per book in the U.S. and 75¢ per book in Canada.* I understand that accepting the 2 free books and gifts places me under no obligation to buy anything. I can always return a shipment and cancel at any time. Even if I never buy another book, the two free books and gifts are mine to keep forever.

235/335 HDN FEGF

| | | |
|---|---|---|
| Name | (PLEASE PRINT) | |
| Address | | Apt. # |
| City | State/Prov. | Zip/Postal Code |

Signature (if under 18, a parent or guardian must sign)

Mail to the **Reader Service:**
**IN U.S.A.:** P.O. Box 1867, Buffalo, NY 14240-1867
**IN CANADA:** P.O. Box 609, Fort Erie, Ontario L2A 5X3

Not valid for current subscribers to Harlequin Special Edition books.

**Want to try two free books from another line?**
**Call 1-800-873-8635 or visit www.ReaderService.com.**

* Terms and prices subject to change without notice. Prices do not include applicable taxes. Sales tax applicable in N.Y. Canadian residents will be charged applicable taxes. Offer not valid in Quebec. This offer is limited to one order per household. All orders subject to credit approval. Credit or debit balances in a customer's account(s) may be offset by any other outstanding balance owed by or to the customer. Please allow 4 to 6 weeks for delivery. Offer available while quantities last.

**Your Privacy**—The Reader Service is committed to protecting your privacy. Our Privacy Policy is available online at www.ReaderService.com or upon request from the Reader Service.

We make a portion of our mailing list available to reputable third parties that offer products we believe may interest you. If you prefer that we not exchange your name with third parties, or if you wish to clarify or modify your communication preferences, please visit us at www.ReaderService.com/consumerchoice or write to us at Reader Service Preference Service, P.O. Box 9062, Buffalo, NY 14269. Include your complete name and address.

HSE1

**Harlequin**

# SPECIAL EDITION

### Life, Love and Family

*USA TODAY* bestselling author

# Marie Ferrarella

### enchants readers in

## ONCE UPON A MATCHMAKER

Micah Muldare's aunt is worried that her nephew is going to wind up alone in his old age...but this matchmaking mama has just the thing! When Micah finds himself accused of theft, defense lawyer Tracy Ryan agrees to help him as a favor to his aunt, but soon finds herself drawn to more than just his case. Will Micah open up his heart and realize Tracy is his match?

*Available June 2012*

Saddle up with Harlequin® series books this summer and find a cowboy for every mood!

*Available wherever books are sold.*

*A grim discovery is about to change everything for
Detective Layne Sullivan—including how she
interacts with her boss!*

*Read on for an exciting excerpt of the upcoming book
UNRAVELING THE PAST by Beth Andrews....*

SOMETHING WAS UP—otherwise why would Chief Ross
Taylor summon her back out? As Detective Layne Sullivan
walked over, she grudgingly admitted he was doing well.
But that didn't change the fact that the Chief position
should have been hers.

Taylor turned as she approached. "Detective Sullivan,
we have a situation."

"What's the problem?"

He aimed his flashlight at the ground. The beam illumi-
nated a dirt-encrusted skull.

"Definitely a problem." And not something she'd expected. Not here. "How'd you see it?"

"Jess stumbled upon it looking for her phone."

Layne looked to where his niece huddled on a log. "I'll
contact the forensics lab."

"Already have a team on the way. I've also called in units
to search for the rest of the remains."

So he'd started the ball rolling. Then, she'd assume command while he took Jess home. "I have this under control."

Though it was late, he was clean shaven and neat, his flat
stomach a testament to his refusal to indulge in doughnuts.
His dark blond hair was clipped at the sides, the top long
enough to curl.

The female part of Layne admitted he was attractive.

The cop in her resented the hell out of him for it.

"You get a lot of missing-persons cases here?" he asked

"People don't go missing from Mystic Point." Although plenty of them left. "But we have our share of crime."

"I'll take the lead on this one."

Bad enough he'd come to *her* town and taken the position she was meant to have, now he wanted to mess with *how* she did her job? "Why? I'm the only detective on third shift and your second in command."

"Careful, Detective, or you might overstep."

But she'd never played it safe.

"I don't think it's overstepping to clear the air. You have something against me?"

"I assign cases based on experience and expertise. You don't have to like how I do that, but if you need to question every decision, perhaps you'd be happier somewhere else."

"Are you threatening my job?"

He moved so close she could feel the warmth from his body. "I'm not threatening anything." His breath caressed her cheek. "I'm giving you the choice of what happens next."

*What will Layne choose? Find out in*
*UNRAVELING THE PAST by Beth Andrews,*
*available June 2012 from Harlequin® Superromance®.*

*And be sure to look for the other two books*
*in Beth's THE TRUTH ABOUT THE SULLIVANS series*
*available in August and October 2012.*

HSREXP0612

**Harlequin® Romance**

A touching new duet from fan-favorite author

# SUSAN MEIER

*First Time DADS!*

When millionaire CEO Max Montgomery spots
Kate Hunter-Montgomery—the wife he's never forgotten—
back in town with a daughter who looks just like him, he's
determined to win her back. But can this savvy business tycoon
convince Kate to trust her a second time with her heart?

*Find out this June in*

## THE TYCOON'S SECRET DAUGHTER

*And look for book 2 coming this August!*

## NANNY FOR THE MILLIONAIRE'S TWINS

Saddle up with Harlequin® series books this summer
and find a cowboy for every mood!